"Here, try a bite."

He opened his mouth a... sweet taste bursting o...

"What do you think?" she asked.

"It's good." He withdrew a clean spoon from the drawer, dipped it into the small mixing bowl and offered it to her. "Your turn."

"Okay." Her mouth opened and closed around the spoon, tasting it herself. Then she ran the tip of her tongue over her lips.

His knees went weak, and an almost overwhelming urge rose up inside, pressing him to take her in his arms and kiss her. But he couldn't do that. He shouldn't anyway, and tamped down the compulsion as best he could.

Still, he continued to study her.

"Hmm, this is really good." Her voice came out soft. Sweet. Smooth.

He couldn't help himself; he reached out and brushed the flour from the tip of her nose.

Desire flared, his heart pumped hard and steady and his hand stilled. The temptation to kiss her senseless rose up again, stronger than ever. But he wouldn't do that.

He shouldn't.

Oh, why the hell not?

ROCKING CHAIR RODEO:
Cowboys—and true love—never go out of style!

Dear Reader,

I love the holidays—and I especially love holiday books and movies. So I'm thrilled to join the Special Edition lineup in November.

In this story, we're going back to the Rocking Chair Ranch, where you'll meet some old friends, like the lovable but sometimes crotchety Rex, as well as a new one—Sully, who'll play Santa Claus at the upcoming Christmas party.

Love is in the air again on the Rocking C. Rodeo promoter Drew Madison arrives for a three-week stay to interview some of the old cowboys for a blog he is writing for Rocking Chair Rodeo. Attraction flares and sparks fly when he crosses paths with the temporary cook, Lainie Montoya, who's recovering from a relationship gone wrong. Little do they know that they share a scandalous past, which will come to a head just before they host a special party to benefit a nearby children's home. Can they put aside past deceit, pain and misunderstandings so that they can embrace a bright and happy future with each other?

Wishing you romance and a cozy holiday season filled with love, laughter and warm, happy memories!

Judy

PS: I love hearing from my readers. You can contact me through my website, judyduarte.com, or on Facebook at Facebook.com/judyduartenovelist.

A Cowboy Family Christmas

Judy Duarte

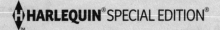

HARLEQUIN® SPECIAL EDITION®

Recycling programs
for this product may
not exist in your area.

ISBN-13: 978-0-373-62382-2

A Cowboy Family Christmas

Copyright © 2017 by Judy Duarte

Printed in U.S.A.

Since 2002, *USA TODAY* bestselling author **Judy Duarte** has written over forty books for Harlequin Special Edition, earned two RITA® Award nominations, won two Maggie Awards and received a National Readers' Choice Award. When she's not cooped up in her writing cave, she enjoys traveling with her husband and spending quality time with her grandchildren. You can learn more about Judy and her books at her website, judyduarte.com, or at Facebook.com/judyduartenovelist.

To my aunties:
Dorothy Johnston Eggleston and Loraine Shaw.
Thank you for your incredible love and support
over the years. I love you both!

Chapter One

Dear Debbie,
I'm desperate and need your help.

Elena Montoya studied the first of several letters she'd been handed during her job interview at *The Brighton Valley Gazette*. She'd come here today, hoping to get her foot in the door at the small-town newspaper, but as a reporter. Not someone offering advice to the lovelorn in a weekly column.

Mr. Carlton, the balding, middle-aged editor, leaned forward, resting clasped hands on his desk. "So what do you think?"

Seriously? Elena would be hard-pressed to offer advice to anyone, especially someone with romantic trouble. But she didn't want to reveal her inexperience or doubt. "I'd hoped to land a different assignment—or another type of column."

"Let's see what you can do with this first." Mr. Carlton leaned back in his desk chair, the springs creaking under his weight, the buttons of his cotton shirt straining to contain his middle-age spread.

Elena knew better than to turn down work, even though this job wasn't a good fit. Worse yet, the pay he'd offered her wasn't enough to cover a pauper's monthly expenses. And since she was new in town, she needed a way to support herself.

But as an advice columnist? The irony was laughable.

"You look a bit…uneasy," the editor said.

She *was*. Either Mr. Carlton had neglected to read her resume or he'd confused her with another applicant.

"It's just that…" She cleared her throat and chose her words carefully. "Well, don't get me wrong. I'm happy to have this position, but I only took two psych courses in college. And since I majored in journalism, I'm more qualified to work as a reporter."

"Don't worry. It shouldn't be too difficult for a young woman like you, Elena."

She cringed at his use of her given name. The last thing she needed was for her new co-workers at the newspaper—or any rodeo fans in the small Texas community—to connect the dots and realize who she was. And why she looked familiar—in spite of her efforts to change her appearance.

"By the way," she said, "I go by Lainie." At least,

that's the childhood nickname her twin sister had given her.

"All right," Mr. Carlton said. "Then *Lainie* it is. But keep in mind you'll be known as 'Dear Debbie' around here. We like her true identity to be a secret."

A temporary secret identity was just what Lainie needed. After that embarrassing evening, when rodeo star Craig Baxter's wife had caught him and Elena together at a hotel restaurant in Houston and assumed the worst, Elena had done her best to lay low. The next day, she'd relocated to a ranch outside of Brighton Valley, where she could hide out until she could rise above those awful rumors—all of which were either untrue or blown way out of proportion.

Elena had tried to explain how she'd come to be there that night—how she had no idea that Craig was a rodeo star, let alone married—to no avail. Kara Baxter had been so angry at her husband, she'd thrown a margarita in Elena's face and read him the riot act. As if that hadn't been bad enough, someone at another table had caught it all on video, and the whole, ugly scene had gone viral. And now Kara's friends and Craig's fans blamed her for splitting up a marriage that wouldn't have lasted anyway.

"Do you have any other questions?" Mr. Carlton asked.

As a matter of fact, she had a ton of them, but she didn't want to show any sign of insecurity.

"I do have one question," she admitted. "Some of the people writing these letters could be dealing with serious issues. And if that's the case, I'm not qualified to offer them any advice." Nor should she counsel anyone, for that matter.

Mr. Carlton shook his head and waved off her concern. "Our last Debbie used to have a stock answer for the bigger problems. She told them to seek professional help."

Lainie nodded. "Okay. Then I'll use that response." A *lot*.

"Just focus on the interesting letters or on those that trigger a clever response," Mr. Carlton said. "It's really just entertainment for most people. But keep in mind, if the readership of the Dear Debbie column increases, I'll give you a bigger assignment in the future."

At least, he'd given her a chance to prove herself, something she'd had to do time and again since the third grade, when she'd gone from a foster home to a pediatric intensive care unit and lost track of her sister. "I'll give it my best shot, Mr. Carlton."

"Okay, kid. What's the best number if I need to get a hold of you?"

"I listed my cell on my resume, although that's not the best way to reach me. I'm temporarily staying at the Rocking Chair Ranch. Since the reception isn't very good there, and the Wi-Fi is worse, you'd better call me on the landline." She pointed to her resume, which he'd set aside on his desk. "I included that number, too, and marked it with an asterisk."

"If you don't mind me asking, why are you staying at a retirement home for old cowboys?"

"Because I'm filling in for the ranch cook, who'll be gone for the next three weeks." When Lainie first heard about the temporary position, she'd declined. But after that awful run-in with Kara Baxter, she'd changed her mind and accepted it out of desperation, realizing it would provide her with a place to stay until she could find something better and more permanent in town.

Oddly enough, she actually felt a lot more comfortable staying at the Rocking C than she'd thought she would. And she liked the old men who lived there. Most of them were sweet, and even the crotchety few were entertaining.

Mr. Carlton pushed back his chair and got to his feet, signaling the interview was over.

Lainie stood, too. Still hoping for something more respectable and better paying, she said, "I minored in photography, so if you need a photojournalist, that's another option."

"I'll keep that in mind. Consider this your trial run, kid."

Lainie nodded and reached for her purse.

Mr. Carlton headed for the door of his office and opened it for her. "I'll send you a copy of the letters electronically, and even if you're somewhere with terrible web access, your column is due by email before midnight on Wednesday. I can't wait to see it."

"You won't be disappointed. I'll channel my inner Debbie." Lainie tamped down her doubt, offered him a smile and lifted the letters in her hand. "You'll love what I do with these."

Mr. Carlton beamed, clearly convinced that she'd work a miracle of some kind, but Lainie knew better.

And she feared that by Friday morning, when her first column came out, her inadequacy would come to light.

Rodeo promoter Drew Madison drove his pickup down the county highway on his way to the Rocking C Ranch, listening to a Brad Paisley hit on the radio and sporting a confident grin. His plans for the Rocking Chair Rodeo were finally coming together, and a date had finally been set. The county-wide event would be held at the Brighton Valley Fairgrounds in April.

Drew's boss at Esteban Enterprises had granted him free rein on the project, although he'd insisted that Drew move in to the Rocking Chair Ranch for a few weeks, interview the old cowboys who lived there and write a few blog posts sharing their stories.

While Drew had graduated from college and certainly knew how to put a sentence together, he'd never considered himself a writer. But his promotion to VP of the company was on the line, so he'd brushed away his doubt and agreed to do it.

Besides, how hard could writing a few stories be?

His cell phone rang, the Bluetooth automatically shutting out the Brad Paisley tune. He assumed it was another business call, but when he looked at the dashboard and spotted his sister's name on the display, his heart clenched.

Kara Lee had been going through a lot lately, so he'd made it a point to check up on her each morning and evening. To have her contact him in the middle of the day was a little unsettling.

He answered quickly and tried to keep his tone upbeat. "Hey, sis. What's up?"

"Not much. I'm just bored, I guess. I called your office, and they said you were traveling. Not that it really matters, but I thought you would've mentioned something about it to me."

He hadn't meant to keep it a secret, but neither had he wanted her to worry about him being gone and unable to get to the hospital in time if she went into labor. She'd nearly lost her baby last week and was on complete bed rest now.

"Actually," he said, "it's a new assignment. I meant to tell you about it, but I had to cut our morning call short."

"How long will you be gone this time?"

Longer than he wanted to admit, although he was looking forward to meeting the retired cowboys. "I'll be gone for a few weeks, but I'm not far from Houston. If you need me, all you have to do is call. I can get there within a couple of hours."

"I'm sure that won't be necessary," she said, but the tone of her voice betrayed her words. "I'll be fine."

He certainly hoped so. Kara Lee had wanted to be a mother for as long as she could cuddle a dolly. And after three miscarriages, she'd made it to the fifth month this time around. For each day the little boy remained in the womb, the better chance he had.

"So where's this assignment?" she asked.

"The Rocking Chair Ranch. The rodeo will be sponsoring them in the spring, so I'm working on the promotion."

"Is that the retirement home for cowboys?"

"And ranchers." He'd been reluctant to mention anything about rodeos or cowboys since the night she found out her husband, rodeo star Craig Baxter, was having another affair. The stress from the confrontation with him and his lover had caused her to go into premature labor.

When Drew got word of the public blowup and learned that Kara Lee had been hospitalized, he'd wanted to beat the tar out of his brother-in-law. But Kara Lee had begged him not to, and he'd been reluctant to do anything to upset his kid sister, especially when the survival of her son was precarious. But that didn't mean he wouldn't be tempted to knock Craig's lights out the next time he saw him.

Kara Lee had told Craig to pack his crap and to get out of the house, which he did. But she hadn't yet filed for divorce, mostly because she wasn't able to deal with the legal proceedings when she was lying flat on her back. But once the baby came, Drew would do whatever he could to facilitate a fair and amicable split. One of his friends was a divorce attorney in Houston, and he'd already mentioned the case to him. He just hoped his sister didn't soften and take Craig back.

"You sure you're okay?" he asked her again.

"Yeah, especially since I've made it to the twenty-sixth week. At least the baby now has a chance to survive."

"That's good to know."

As silence filled the line, he decided to change the subject. "So what are you doing?" The moment the question rolled off his tongue, he wanted to reel it back in. Hell, what could a bedridden pregnant woman possibly do, other than read or watch TV?

She let out a sigh. "I wish I could work on the nursery, but I'll have to wait until after little Robby gets here."

"I'll tell you what," Drew said. "As soon as I finish this project at the Rocking C, I'll spend a few days at your place. Make a Pinterest board of stuff you like. When I get back, I'll be your hands and feet. We'll have it done before you know it."

"I love you, Drew."

"Aw, for Pete's sake. Don't get all sappy on me, Kara Lee." She'd been a tomboy when growing up—and a barrel racer in high school. So he wasn't used to seeing her softer side. It must be her hormones.

"You're the best, Drew."

"No. I'm not." He'd taken on a demanding job that required him to travel, so he hadn't been there for her recently, like he'd always been in the past.

He kicked himself for that now. If he'd been around more, he might have talked her out of marrying Craig. But that was all muddy water under the bridge now. From here on out, Drew was going to be the brother she deserved.

If Kara Lee suffered yet another miscarriage, losing the baby she'd already named and loved, there was no telling what it would do to her.

"By the way," he said. "I called an agency that provides home health services and asked them to send someone out to your house for a few hours each day.

She'll do some light cleaning and run errands for you while I'm gone."

"You didn't need to do that."

"I know, but I wanted to. It makes me feel better to know someone is with you or at least just a phone call away." He thought she might object, more out of pride than anything else. But she surprised him by accepting his effort to help.

"You know what, Drew? You're going to make some woman a wonderful husband."

He laughed. "My last two relationships didn't fare very well, thanks to all my travel." Well, that and the fact that he was beginning to enjoy being a tumbleweed, rolling through life on the whim of the wind.

Just like your old man? He winced, then discarded the thought as quickly as it came. He wasn't at all like his father.

"Besides," he added, "I'm not cut out for marriage, family or a home in the suburbs. If I was, I wouldn't enjoy being on the road so often."

"A woman who really loves you wouldn't complain about you being gone."

"I don't know about that. You'd be surprised."

"At least, you'd never cheat on her." She paused for a beat. "You wouldn't *cheat*, would you?"

"*Me?* No, I've always been honest with the women I date. From the very first time we go out, I make it clear that I'm not the domestic type."

"I'm not buying that," Kara Lee said.

Drew wasn't about to let his little sister psychoanalyze him. Who knew what assumptions she'd come to, right or wrong.

When he spotted the big yellow sign that indicated he'd reached the Rocking C, he said, "Listen, I have to hang up now. But I'll give you a call this evening."

"You don't have to. I know how busy you are."

"I'm never too busy for you."

And that was the truth. Kara Lee was the only family Drew had left, and after all they'd been through, especially *her*, she deserved to be happy—and to finally be a mom.

"I'm curious," she said. "Where will you be staying while on the ranch?"

"They're putting me up in one of the cabins so I can get a feel for the daily routine. It's not just a retirement home, it's a working ranch. So the whole enterprise is new and innovative. I'd like to check it out."

"Good luck."

"Thanks. I'm actually looking forward to having a change of pace—and to being in the same place for longer than a few days."

"So says the family rover. Maybe you're more cut out for home and hearth than you think, especially if you meet the right woman."

"Oh, yeah? We'll see about that." Drew turned onto the long, graveled drive that led to the Rocking Chair Ranch. "I'll talk to you later."

When the line disconnected, he slowly shook his head. If there was one thing he'd learned over his thirty-one years, it was easier to be a rover than to deal with the countless people who weren't what they seemed and were bound to disappoint you.

Thank goodness he wasn't likely to meet any of that type on the Rocking C.

It had been two days since Mr. Carlton had hired Lainie to write the Dear Debbie column, but she still hadn't made any headway in answering a single letter.

She'd been busy settling into her temporary job. But that wasn't the whole story. In fact, none of the problems of people seeking Debbie's advice had triggered a clever or witty response, and Lainie was stumped.

She sat at the kitchen table, reading through the letters, trying to choose an interesting one or two to include in her first Dear Debbie column. While she pondered, her fingers tapped softly on the keyboard without typing out a single word. She glanced at the clock on the microwave, noting how much time had passed since she'd done the breakfast dishes, and blew out a sigh. Her midnight deadline loomed.

"You can do this," she whispered aloud. Then she reread the letter on top of the stack.

Last year, I met John, the most handsome, amazing man in the world, and I knew I'd finally met Mr. Right.

Last month, Lainie had met Craig…

Darn it. She had to stop projecting that jerk into each of these stupid letters written by someone who'd either been jilted or disappointed by various people in their lives.

All I've ever wanted was to fall in love and get married, but now my heart is broken, and my life is a wreck.

"Tell me about it," Lainie muttered. Well, not the broken heart. She'd gone out with Craig only three times, but the rest of it sounded pretty darned familiar.

Then, a few weeks ago, a woman who works at John's office started hitting on him and lured him away from me.

Lainie leaned back in the chair and shook her head. From the comments left on the YouTube video of her that night at the Houston hotel, it seemed everyone in the rodeo world thought she'd targeted a married man and tried to lure him away.

During the blowup, his wife had told him off, implying that he was a serial cheater, a secret he apparently kept from his legion of fans.

"Aw, come on," Lainie scolded herself. "Focus on *this* woman, *this* letter, *this* problem."

Yet how could she? She was the last person in the world who should offer romantic advice to anyone, let alone a stranger who hoped for an easy fix.

Darn it. No matter how badly she'd wanted a job at the *Gazette*—and she *needed* one if she wanted to support herself—she'd been crazy to agree to taking over for Dear Debbie.

Footsteps sounded in the doorway, drawing her from her reading. She glanced up to see Otis "Sully" Sullivan enter the kitchen. The sweet, kindhearted old man had a jolly way about him. Each time she laid eyes on the retired cowboy, she couldn't help but smile. With a head of thick white hair and a full beard, he reminded her of Santa Claus, especially today when he wore a solid red flannel shirt.

"Hey, Sully."

"I'm sorry to bother you, but is there any more coffee?"

Lainie set aside the letter she'd been reading, pushed back her chair and got to her feet. "It's no bother at all. And you're in luck. There's still at least a cup left."

She poured the last of the carafe into a white mug. "I could make a fresh pot."

"No need for you to go to any extra trouble." Sully took the mug she gave him, gripping it with gnarled hands, and thanked her. "That was a nice breakfast you fixed us today. I haven't had good chilaquiles in a long time. My late wife used to make them for me every Sunday morning, but she usually overcooked them."

Lainie laughed. "Did she? How were mine?"

"Best I've ever had. Nice, crispy tortillas. Perfectly scrambled eggs. Mmm, mmm, mmm."

Lainie beamed at the compliment. She wasn't used to getting many. "Thanks, I'm glad you liked them. When I was a little girl, my grandmother used to make them for me and my sister."

"You got a sister?"

"Yes, a twin."

Sully brightened. "Where is she?"

Lainie had no idea. The two of them had been sepa-rated years ago, when Lainie had been taken from the group home and sent to the hospital to be treated for an undetected congenital heart defect. It had taken a while for the doctors to decide upon a treatment plan, and by the time Lainie recovered from her lifesaving surgery, a couple arrived at the children's home, adopted the healthy girl and left the sickly one behind. From what Lainie had gathered, her sister's new parents had been afraid to assume financial responsibility of a child with such serious medical issues.

As a result, she hadn't seen her twin since, but she offered Sully the happy outcome she'd imagined for Erica. "She's happily married to her high school sweet-heart and has a two-year-old daughter."

Before Sully could press further, Lainie turned the conversation back to the chilaquiles. "Anyway, my grandmother passed away before she could pass on her recipe. But when I got older, I did some research and a little experimenting until I came up with a batch that tasted nearly as good as hers. I hope they weren't too spicy."

"No," he said, "not at all. The salsa was perfect. In fact, that was one of the tastiest meals I've had since I moved in here. Not that Joy, our regular cook, isn't a good one, but she's more of a down-home, meat-and-potatoes gal. And I like good Mexican food once in a while."

"That's a relief. I knew I'd have some big shoes to fill, taking Joy's place in the kitchen while she's on her honeymoon."

"I haven't heard any complaints yet. And that's saying a lot, considering some of the old geezers who live here. They rarely keep their opinions to themselves." Sully glanced at the letters on the table. "I didn't mean to bother you. I'll just take my coffee into the living room and let you get back to whatever it was you were doing."

"Actually, I don't mind the interruption." Although she really should. With each tick and tock of the kitchen clock, her midnight deadline drew closer. And who knew if the ranch internet would work? She might have to drive into town and find Wi-Fi somewhere. *Darn it*.

"You look fretful, which doesn't do your pretty face any good. What's bothering you?" Sully nodded toward the stack of letters. "I hope it isn't bad news."

"It's just…a friend with a problem." Lainie chewed her fingernail and stared at the pile of unanswered letters. "I'm trying to come up with some wise advice, but I'm not feeling very wise."

Sully's smile softened the lines in his craggy face. "Wisdom comes with age and experience. Back when I was in my twenties, heck, thirties, too, I was under the false notion that I was as smart as I'd ever get."

Lainie had thought the same thing after her college graduation, which wasn't very long ago. Then Craig had taken her for a ride, leaving her with an unearned bad reputation and distrustful of sweet-talking men who couldn't tell the truth to save their souls. She'd learned a big lesson the hard way, but that hadn't made her an expert at facing romantic dilemmas.

"Want me to give it a shot?" Sully asked.

Was he offering his advice? Lainie wasn't sure what the dear old man might have to say, but at this point, she'd take all the help she could get. "Sure, if you don't mind."

Sully pulled out a chair, took a seat and rested his steaming hot mug on the table. "What's the problem?"

Lainie scanned the opening of the letter and caught him up to speed, revealing that her "friend" was twenty-four years old, relatively nice-looking with a decent job and a good sense of humor. Then she read the rest of it out loud.

"Three weeks ago, I found out the guy I was living with, the man of my dreams, was seeing another woman. We had a big fight, and he moved out. I've been crying every day, and I'm desperate to win him back."

Sully clucked his tongue. "A man who cheats on his partner, romantic or otherwise, isn't a prize worth winning back. That's what I'd tell her."

Lainie had once thought Craig was a prize, and boy, had she been wrong about that. It's a shame she hadn't had Sully nearby when she'd been taken in by that liar's soft Southern drawl. But Sully was here now. And providing the wisdom this letter writer needed.

"That's a good point," Lainie said. It was clever, too, and a good response for the column. "I'll mention that to…my friend."

Male voices sounded outside, growing louder until

the mudroom door squeaked open. A second later, Nate Gallagher, the acting foreman, entered the kitchen.

Sully acknowledged Nate with a nod, but Lainie focused on the man walking behind him. She guessed him to be a rancher or horseman, since his stylish Western wear suggested he could afford to hire someone to do the dirty work. He was in his early to midthirties, tall and nice looking, with broad shoulders and a rugged build.

He removed his black Stetson, revealing sandy-blond hair, which he wore longer than most of the rodeo cowboys she'd met. Not that she'd ever been a buckle bunny or even attracted to that kind of guy before she'd met Craig.

And after that awful night, she'd sworn off men indefinitely. Yet she found herself stirred by this one's presence. He also looked familiar. Had she met him before?

"Meet Drew Madison," Nate said. "He's handling the Rocking Chair Rodeo promotion."

Just the word *rodeo* sent Lainie's heart slamming into her chest. Had she seen him while on one of the few dates she'd had with Craig?

No, she'd never forget a man like him.

But if he and Craig ran in the same circles, he might recognize *her*. For that reason, she'd better get out of here. She didn't mind being around the older cowboys, some of whom had ridden in the rodeo back in the days before cable television and social media. But a recent connection spelled trouble—and further humiliation.

Nevertheless, she wouldn't be rude to a ranch visitor. So she placed the letter she'd been holding upside down on the rest of the stack on the table. Then she got to her feet and said, "It's nice to meet you. I'll put on a pot of coffee."

Then she did just that. If there was one thing she'd learned in her short time at the Rocking C, it was that the cowboys, young and old, loved a fresh brew.

As the coffee began to perk, Lainie studied the pot as if it might bounce off the countertop if she didn't stand guard.

She fingered the side of her head, checking to see if any strands had come loose. She used to wear it long, the curls tumbling along her shoulders and down her back. But after that video had gone viral, she'd pulled it up into a prim topknot—just one of several alterations she'd made to her appearance so she could fade into the background until that ugly incident was forgotten.

When the coffeemaker let out a last steamy gurgle, she poured two cups, then turned to face the younger men. They continued to stand in the middle of the kitchen, speaking to Sully, who was still seated at the table. She was about to excuse herself and leave them to chat among themselves, but her curiosity betrayed her and she took one last glace at Drew, who'd zeroed in on her.

"For some reason," he said, his gaze intense enough to see right through her, "it seems as if I've met you before."

"That's not likely," she said. "I'm not from around here."

"Where are you from?"

She wanted to ask, *What's up with the third degree?* Instead, she said, "I'm from up north—originally. But I'm sure we've never met. I just have that kind of face. I get comments like that all the time. Sugar? Cream?"

"I like it black."

His gaze continued to roam over her, as if removing her façade one piece at a time. But she pushed through the discomfort and handed him a mug.

He thanked her but didn't take a drink. Instead, those baby blues continued to study her as if trying to pinpoint where they'd met. But wouldn't she remember if they had? A woman wouldn't forget a man like him.

No, he was mistaken. She glanced down at the loose blouse and baggy jeans she wore today. She hadn't used any makeup. Her curls had been pulled into a bun.

But when she again looked at him, when their gazes locked, her heart soared and her hormones flared. For a moment she wished she'd been wearing that red dress Craig had given her for her birthday and insisted that she wear to the hotel that night, their first significant date, where they were to celebrate by having dinner. But she suspected someone who frequented thrift shops had already snatched it up, pleased with their find.

"If you'll excuse me," Lainie said, "I have work to do."

Then she left the kitchen and headed for her room.

After that awful night in Houston, she'd made up her mind to steer clear of handsome cowboys. And Drew Madison was as handsome as any cowboy she'd ever seen.

Chapter Two

Drew leaned back in his chair and watched the house-keeper stride toward the kitchen doorway. She wasn't the kind of woman he usually found attractive, but for some reason he did, and he hadn't been able to keep his eyes off her.

She had a wholesome, clean-cut way about her. Maybe it was the lack of makeup, which she really didn't need. She looked cute in those baggy overalls and plain white T-shirt, but there seemed to be real beauty underneath.

Her dark hair had been pulled up in a simple top-knot, but he imagined it'd be lush and glossy if she wore it loose. And those brown, soulful eyes? A man could get lost in them.

She'd said they'd never met, and she was probably

right. Her name didn't ring a bell. Laney? It wasn't one you heard every day.

Even though she'd already stepped out of the kitchen, he continued to watch the open doorway until Nate mentioned Drew's sister.

"How's Kara Lee doing?" he said. "It must have been devastating for her to lose another baby."

"She's still pregnant, thank goodness."

"Really?" Nate said. "That's good news. I'd heard otherwise, which would have been a real shame."

"There're a lot of rumors going around." Hell, Drew had heard most of them.

"Speaking of babies," Drew said. "How's little Jessica?"

Nate, who'd recently assumed custody of his newborn daughter, a preemie, broke into a proud papa grin. "She's doing great—and growing like a weed."

"And Anna?"

Nate's smile deepened. "She's the best thing that ever happened to me. I love being married."

"Better you than me," Drew said.

Nate chuckled. "Anyway, I'm glad Kara Lee's doing all right."

"Part of what you heard was true," Nate said. "She did go into labor the night she caught Craig cheating. Thankfully, her obstetrician managed to stop the contractions, but she's on bed rest for the time being."

"That's got to be tough," Nate said. "Especially for an active woman like her."

"You got that right, she's determined to have this baby. And she'll do whatever it takes."

"Well, give her my best," Nate said. "I know how badly she wants a kid."

"This one's a boy. And she plans to name him Robert. Bobby for short."

"I hate to even bring up his name, but how's Craig fit into the picture? I heard he's been begging her to forgive him."

Drew's back stiffened. "Where did you hear that?"

"Just around. There's been a lot of talk."

Drew wished that was one rumor he could debunk, but it was true. Craig had been calling her, promising her the moon. "I can't see her taking him back. Hell, I wouldn't be surprised if he was still seeing that sexy brunette who was with him in that hotel restaurant."

"Knowing Craig like I do, you're probably right." Nate crossed his arms. "I didn't see the video, but a couple of the other guys working here did. They say that woman looked like a pop-star wannabe. Did you see it?"

"Yeah." Way too many times. "I didn't get a clear look at her face, but she was certainly dressed the part in that curve-hugging red dress and high heels."

Other than that, Drew didn't know much about the woman, other than what he'd either heard through the rodeo grapevine or gathered from social media. Rumor had it her name was Elena, that she knew how to get what she wanted and that she'd set her sights on landing a champion bull rider, even if he was married to someone else.

Now there was another person he'd like to confront— if he ever crossed paths with her.

Kara Lee had told him that the brunette had claimed it was all a mistake, that Kara Lee had it all wrong. But there were plenty of nearby bars and restaurants where that woman and Craig could have met. So there was only one reason for them to be at a hotel.

Nate clucked his tongue and shook his head. "Craig never did deserve a woman like Kara Lee. And she sure as hell didn't deserve the way he treated her."

"You got that right."

As they both pondered the truth of that fact, the room grew silent for a couple of beats. Then Sully spoke up and snagged Drew's attention.

"Where did you two fellas meet?" Sully asked.

Drew glanced first at the retired cowboy, then at his buddy. "Nate and I competed in the junior rodeo as kids, and we went to the same high school. But when I left for college, I quit the circuit."

"I never could figure out why," Nate said. "Drew was always the guy to beat. He might not look it now, in those fancy duds and shiny new boots, but he's a damn good cowboy."

Drew shrugged off his friend's compliment, as well as the good-humored ribbing about his success in the business world. "Yep, don't mess with my hair."

They all laughed, but Drew suspected all the rodeo talk struck a tender spot in Nate, who'd suffered a career-ending injury and hadn't had an option when it came to hanging up his spurs.

"Do you guys miss the rodeo?" Sully asked. "I sure did when I had to give it up. But we all have to do that at some point. Our bones don't stay young forever."

Nate shrugged. "Sure, I miss it. I loved the thrill of competition. But now I've got a beautiful wife and baby, and they're more important to me than anything. I actually enjoy being at home these days." He winked at Drew. "Maybe you should consider finding a nice woman and settling down."

"You sound like Kara Lee, but I don't see that lifestyle in my future." He hadn't seen it in his past, either. He and his sister had grown up on their mother's run-down spread outside of Brighton Valley, and the only real memories they'd had consisted of hard work and sparse meals.

"Well, fellas," Sully said, "if you'll excuse me, I think I'll go check the football spreads. A couple of the guys have a Last Man Standing pool, and I'm still in contention."

"Not me," Nate said. "I had to drop out during the second week."

As Sully left the room, chuckling at his good fortune, Nate turned to Drew and pushed away from the table. "I've got to get back to work. I'll let you get started on that interview process. It'll be lunchtime before we know it."

Speaking of lunch, Drew wondered when the cook would be back to start the food prep. He'd like to see her again. Maybe he'd ask again where they might have crossed paths.

It really didn't matter, he supposed. Yet for some weird reason, it did.

Lainie had barely gotten to her room when she realized she'd left those darn Dear Debbie letters on the table. Sure, she'd turned them face-side down, but what if...?

Darn it. The last thing in the world she wanted was for someone on the ranch to see them. So, in spite of her plan to avoid Drew Madison while he was visiting, she hurried back to the kitchen.

She'd no more than entered the room when Drew pulled out a chair and took a seat at the table, right in front of those blasted letters. He placed his hand on them, pushing them aside, and her breath caught.

She'd better move quickly. All she needed was for him—or *anyone*—to learn that she was the new love-lorn columnist, especially since Mr. Carlton wanted Dear Debbie's identity to remain secret. Besides, Lainie wasn't looking forward to adding any failed journalism jobs to her resume.

So she scooped them up, clutching them to her chest. "Let me get rid of this mess for you."

She was about to dash out of the kitchen again when Nate said, "Lainie, you'll need to set out an extra plate for meals for the next few weeks."

"Sure, I can do that. But who...?" She paused, afraid to pose the question when she was already connecting the dots.

"Drew will be staying with us for a little while," Nate said. "He wants to interview the men who live here. Get to know them. Learn their daily routines. I think there's at least one empty cabin that's decent. I'm not sure what's available, but I know Joy gave you a tour of the ranch before she and Sam left on their honeymoon."

If you could call it a tour. Joy had taken Lainie on a quick walk and pointed out a few buildings, none of which she thought would be her concern for the short time she'd be here. But if Drew was going to stay on the Rocking C, she'd take him out to the cabin that was the farthest from the kitchen.

"Of course," she said. "I'll make sure it's aired out and ready for him."

"I hate to inconvenience you," Drew said, his gaze unwavering and kicking her pulse up another notch.

"It's not a problem." She feigned a lighthearted grin and tamped down whatever nervous energy he provoked, either through guilt or fear…or downright sexual attraction. "I'll take care of that cabin right away."

When Nate nodded, Lainie took her chance to escape.

"If you men will excuse me," she said, "I have chores to do." Then she headed toward the living area, clutching the letters to her chest.

As she reached the doorway, she overheard Nate say, "I've gotta get back to work. Next time you talk to Kara Lee, give her my best."

Kara?

Lainie nearly stumbled at the mention of a name that sounded similar to that of Craig's wife. Then she shook it off.

Boy, she was jumpy today. Nate had said Carolee. Or possibly Carrie Leigh. Either way, they surely weren't the same woman.

Thank goodness for that. If Kara Baxter was Drew Madison's friend, and if he realized who Lainie was and believed what people said about her, then having him on the ranch would be a lot more than an inconvenience.

It would be a humiliating disaster.

Lainie had no more than returned from Caroline's Diner, where she'd accessed the free Wi-Fi and emailed her first column to the editor, when she spotted Drew and Nate leaving the barn and heading for the house.

Her pride and enthusiasm waned, and her steps, once light and quick, slowed to a near stop. Her first impulse was to slip into the kitchen before they spotted her, but she couldn't very well do that, even if she did have the dinner meal to prepare.

The men waved to her, and she made her way toward them as if it was the most natural thing in the world to do and greeted them with a forced smile.

"There's the lady we've been looking for," Nate said. "Have you had a chance to get one of the cabins ready for Drew?"

Oops. Her first priority had been to make her deadline—well before the midnight cutoff. She lifted her hand to her throat and fingered the ribbed neckline on her T-shirt, as well as the bib of her overalls, both of which covered the long, thick scar that ran the length of her sternum. "I haven't made up the bed yet, but the cabin on the knoll behind the barn will work best. It's empty, and I'm pretty sure it's clean."

"Do you have time to check on it now?" Nate asked. "I'm sure Drew would like to get settled in before dinner, if possible."

Lainie was already behind schedule, but she couldn't shirk her responsibilities, especially when this job paid her a lot more than the newspaper did. "Of course. Just give me a minute to get fresh linens and a set of towels from the house."

"Thanks," Nate said. "I'd do it myself, but I'm going to be tied up for a while."

Lainie shot a quick glance at Drew, who was perusing her every bit as intently as he'd done before. Why did he keep doing that?

Her hand began to reach for her chest again, but she let it drop, her fingers trailing along the denim and brushing away imaginary dust. The scar wasn't visible, and she had to stop reverting back to the old habit she'd once kicked.

"I'll see you at dinner," Nate told Drew. "I need to have a chat with a couple of hands who are at odds with each other. It seems they're both dating the same cocktail waitress at the Stagecoach Inn. I couldn't care less what they do with their time off, but it's begun to affect their work."

"The woes of being a supervisor," Drew said.

Nate rolled his eyes. "That's *acting* supervisor. And you're right. It's not an easy job, especially with a young and inexperienced crew. Once Sam gets back from his honeymoon, I'm going to turn over my keys to the ranch and hightail it out of here."

"We're looking forward to having you join us at Esteban Enterprises," Drew said.

"I'm glad to hear that, because I can't wait." The

guys did some elaborate hand shake and fist pump ritual.

Lainie planned to move on once the honeymooners returned, too. Only problem was, she didn't have another job lined up, like Nate did.

Nate would undoubtedly be successful at Esteban Enterprises, but Lainie'd hate to work for a company that had anything to do with rodeos. Cowboys weren't her thing—except maybe for Sully and the other oldsters. But she'd prefer to never cross paths with the younger ones again.

She glanced at the handsome promoter. Drew might be dressed like a fancy Texas businessman, but his more casual demeanor shouted urban cowboy. So the sooner she could escort him to his temporary quarters and be done with it, the better off she'd be.

"I'll go inside for the linens," she told him. "Do you have your bags?"

"Just a suitcase and my briefcase. They're in the back of my pickup. It'll only take me a minute."

"Then I'll meet you back here."

Moments later, with her arms laden with freshly laundered sheets, pillowcases and towels, Lainie returned to the yard and found Drew waiting for her. He held a suitcase in one hand and a leather briefcase in the other.

"There it is." She pointed about fifty yards away from the barn, where a lone structure sat. The outside needed a coat or two of paint, but the inside was probably just fine. It looked sturdy enough and should keep him dry and cozy. "It doesn't look like much, but I think you'll be comfortable there."

"I don't require much."

No? She found that hard to believe. She glanced across the driveway at his spanking new Dodge Ram truck, then at his fancy denim jacket, his silver belt buckle and his shiny leather inlaid boots. No, this guy clearly liked the finer things in life.

"This way." She began walking along the graveled path toward the knoll, and he fell into step beside her.

"There's something you should know," she said. "The cell and internet access on the ranch isn't very good. There are some random spots here and there where you might get a bar or two, but it's sketchy at best."

"I won't need to get online right away."

"Okay, but when you do, it might be easier and faster to drive to town. Caroline's Diner offers free Wi-Fi now. And they also have the best desserts you've ever tasted."

"Thanks for the suggestion. I'll keep that in mind."

They turned to the right, following the incline to the cabin. A cool winter breeze kicked up a bit, sending the scent of his cologne her way. It was a clean woodsy fragrance—no doubt expensive—that suited him.

For a moment, her femininity rebelled, scolding her for not applying makeup earlier this morning, for choosing a plain white T-shirt and baggy overalls. But her days of enhancing her curves—whether they could be considered a blessing or a curse—were behind her now.

Yet despite her resolve to remain low-key and unaffected by Drew's presence, she stole a peek at him, hoping he wouldn't notice. But he caught her in the act. Her cheeks warmed, and she quickly looked away, placing her focus on the pathway.

"Have you ever been to Houston?" he asked.

The first image that flashed in her mind was the swanky hotel restaurant, where Craig had invited her for a birthday dinner. But she shook off the memory the best she could. "I went to college in Houston, but I'm originally from Amarillo."

He nodded, as if storing that tidbit of information away to use against her someday. *No, come on. That kind of thinking is crazy.* But she couldn't help being a wee bit suspicious. For some reason, he seemed to have locked onto the idea that they'd met before, and they hadn't. She was sure of it.

Still, there seemed to be something familiar about him. Probably his lanky, cowboy swagger.

She cut a sideways glance his way. "Why do you ask?"

"Just curious about everyone here."

She reminded herself that she'd have to stay on her toes around him.

They approached the small front porch, which appeared to have a rickety railing. Maybe the cabin wasn't so sturdy after all, but it would have to do.

"This is it," she said, hoping the inside was more appealing than the outside. "I probably should have checked things out before bringing you here."

"All I need is a place to sleep."

Lainie climbed the three steps ahead of him, when a crack and crunch sounded behind her.

"Dammit." Drew lurched forward and, apparently to steady himself, grabbed her hip, sending a spiral of heat to the bone and unbalancing her, too.

She didn't have to turn around to know what had just happened, but she couldn't help herself. Sure enough, he was removing his foot from a big crack in the wood, scratching his fancy boots in the process and banging his fancy leather suitcase against the steps.

He grumbled something she couldn't comprehend, then removed his hand from her denim-clad hip. Yet her skin sizzled from his touch, tingled from his grip.

"I'm sorry," she said. "I didn't realize that step was loose."

"The wood's completely rotten."

"I can see that. I know the owners plan to refurbish the cabins before the rodeo comes to town, but I don't think there's a lot of extra cash right now. Are you okay?"

Their gazes locked, and her pulse struck a wacky beat. His features softened, and his annoyance disappeared.

"Yeah, I'm fine. But this porch needs to be fixed pronto."

"I agree, but I think a repair like that'll have to wait."

"Seriously?" He straightened and slowly stepped onto the porch, testing the wood before placing his full weight on it. "Fixing that step can't wait. I might break my leg next time."

She clutched the linens to her chest. "Good point. But...like I said, Nate can't spare the extra cash right now."

He shrugged a single shoulder. "I'll fix it myself. I'm not too bad with a hammer and nails. Tomorrow morning, I'll go to the hardware store and get supplies I'll need to rebuild the broken step." He glanced around. "And the porch. It's just a matter of time before it falls apart, too."

"You're taking it upon yourself to do that?"

"I may as well pay for my keep."

"That'd be nice of you. And appreciated." For some reason, she hadn't expected him to actually do any physical labor. He didn't look like the kind of man who'd risk getting blisters or building up a sweat.

Lainie turned back to face the entrance and shuffled the linen to one arm. She reached for the knob and opened the door. As she crossed the threshold, into the tidy and modestly furnished interior, she caught a whiff of must and dust. "I guess we'd better open some windows and air it out."

"That's not a problem." Drew followed her inside. He set his suitcase on the hardwood floor near the small green-plaid sofa and his briefcase on the oak coffee table.

Lainie carried the linens to the bed and placed them on the bare mattress. Then she took the towels and washcloths to the bathroom. When she returned to the bedroom, she found Drew opening the window. He looked especially nice from the backside—broad shoulders, narrow hips...

Enough of that. Drew Madison was a cowboy—fancy duds or not. And what was worse, Lainie hadn't lucked out when it came to assessing the characters of men she found attractive.

"The pillows, blanket and spread must be in the closet," she said.

"I can take care of that. I'm sure you have other things to do."

She had a ton to do before her day ended. When she'd checked her email at Caroline's, Mr. Carlton had forwarded the next batch of Dear Debbie letters. But Nate had asked her to help their guest get settled. It wouldn't be right to take off and leave him on his own.

"No, I—" She'd just slid open the small closet door, when a brown furry streak jumped from the top shelf, landing on her head. She screamed and swiped at her hair to no avail. The damned creature dropped to her chest and scampered under the bib of her overalls. She shrieked again, and Drew was at her side in an instant.

"What's wrong?" he asked. "Are you okay?"

"No!" She continued to scream and shudder. She hopped up and down in an attempt to dislodge it, but it scurried around her waist and into her pant leg. She grabbed Drew's arm as if he could save her.

His brow furrowed, his expression one of concern. "What? What is it?"

"It's a mouse. And it ran down my…" *Oh, my God.* It was still in there, trying to find a hiding place.

A childhood memory replayed in her mind—the abandoned warehouse in their run-down neighborhood, the innocent game of hide-and-seek, the rat's nest that turned into a little girl's worst nightmare…

Lainie let go of Drew, who wasn't any help, unhooked the overall buckles and shimmied out of the baggy britches until they bagged at her ankles. She struggled to kick off her laced shoes.

"How can I help?" he asked.

If she wasn't in the midst of a mind-boggling crisis, she might have offered a suggestion. But all she could think to do was to scream yet again.

The nasty little creature was burrowing into the folds of the fabric, squirming to escape almost as frantically as she was. When she finally tugged off her second shoe and stepped out of the overalls, she turned to Drew and pointed at the pile of denim. "Get it. Take it *outside*."

Drew bent to do as she'd instructed, but not before the mangy little beast took the opportunity to zip under the bed.

Lainie shuddered and straightened, then she turned to him.

He stood there stoically, his gaze on her. Apparently, he didn't give a fig about the mouse that could easily burrow into his bed tonight.

He studied her for a couple of beats, then he looked away.

It took her those same beats and another to realize she was standing before him in her stocking feet, wearing only a baggy T-shirt and a pair of pink panties. And skimpy ones at that.

Her cheeks heated and her lips parted. Oh, no. Now what?

Drew snatched a folded sheet from the mattress and held it out to her.

She grabbed it and rushed to the bathroom, but it wasn't the blasted mouse she hoped to escape this time. It was the dashing cowboy who'd seen more of her than she'd wanted to reveal.

Chapter Three

Now that the crisis was over, some men might have found Lainie's reaction to a panicked field mouse a bit comical, but Drew had been too focused on her shapely, bare legs and those pink lacy panties. He hadn't realized what she'd been hiding behind all that denim, but certainly not curves that were that sexy.

Most women would flaunt them, but apparently Lainie didn't.

When the bathroom door creaked open, she came out with the sheet wrapped around her waist. Her cheeks were flushed a deep pink, and her brow was creased in worry. She scanned the room. "Is it gone?"

No, he suspected the critter was still under the bed and probably suffering from a massive coronary. He didn't want to lie, but neither did he want to risk having her freak out again. "You're safe."

Drew thought about making light of the situation and her reaction, but she was undoubtedly embarrassed by it. And he couldn't help sympathizing.

She pointed to the pile of denim on the floor. "Would you please shake those out, then give them to me?"

"Sure." He picked up the overalls, made an effort to examine them carefully, then gave them a vigorous shake before handing them to her. "Here you go."

It was a shame she was going to hide behind baggy clothes again.

She held the sheet in place with one hand and clutched the overalls with the other. Yet she stood her ground, her cheeks rosy, and gave a little shrug. "In case you hadn't figured it out, I hate mice."

"Apparently so." His grin broadened to a full-on smile. "But just for future reference, it wasn't going to eat you in a single bite."

She mumbled something directed at him, clicked her tongue then returned to the bathroom.

When the bathroom door swung open again, and she walked out wearing those damned overalls, he felt compelled to tease her. Instead, he bit his tongue. But he couldn't wipe the smile off his face.

"I realize you found this funny," she said, "and I admit that I overreacted."

"No," he lied. "Some people have an aversion to things like mice, bugs and snakes." He took a seat on the bed.

"And I'm one of them. But you see, one day, when

my twin sister and I were playing, we had a bad experience with rats. So that came into play just now."

"You have a twin?"

She paused a beat, and her eye twitched, just as it had a few minutes ago, when he'd asked her if she'd ever been to Houston. "Yes, I do."

"Identical?"

"No. People used to think we were, especially since there's a strong family resemblance and we were the same size and had the same coloring. But no, we're fraternal twins."

Had Drew run into her sister before? If so, that could be the reason Lainie seemed familiar.

"Where does your sister live?" he asked.

"I'm…not sure. I haven't seen her since… Well, it's been a while."

He was tempted to ask why, but he suspected they'd had a falling-out of some kind. And he'd had enough drama within his own family to last a lifetime.

"Anyway," Lainie said, "I need to go back to the house. I only have an hour to get dinner on the table."

"You sure you're okay?"

"I'll live. I'm just glad you reminded me that the darned critter wasn't able to eat me in a single bite." She smiled and winked. Then she bit down on her bottom lip. "Hey, do me a favor, please. Don't tell the guys about this."

"My lips are sealed. It'll be our little secret." This time, he winked. "Thanks for helping me get settled."

"And for providing you with a little entertainment?

You're welcome. I was just doing my job. Or trying to, anyway." Then she headed for the door.

He nearly added, *And thanks for the lovely vision I'll never get out of my head.*

Lainie had never been so embarrassed in her life. She couldn't believe she'd screamed like a wild woman and stripped down to her panties in front of a virtual stranger—and a handsome one at that.

So much for getting a fresh start in Brighton Valley. If word of this got out, she'd have to move again. Fortunately, Drew had been nice about the whole thing, but he must think she was a nut job, which she probably was. What normal woman would have reacted like that? And all because of a tiny little mouse.

She blew out an exasperated sigh. As much as she'd like to avoid Drew for the rest of her life—or at least, for the duration of his stay—she was going to have to face him again this evening, at the dinner table. And speaking of dinner, she didn't have a clue what she was going to fix. She'd been so focused on getting her column turned in on time that she'd neglected to do any prep work. And now she'd have to regroup and think of something that was quick and easy.

She had ground beef in the fridge. Hamburgers with all the fixings wouldn't be too difficult to pull off. By the time she'd gotten across the yard and near the house, she had a menu planned. Thank goodness for the canned beans in the pantry and the ice cream she'd stored in the freezer.

She'd no more than reached the back porch of the

main ranch house when she spotted Sully and Rex, another old-timer, sitting outside, swaying away the afternoon in rocking chairs. They were watching—or rather critiquing—a younger cowboy working with a horse in the corral.

"Damn fool kid," Rex said. "Someone had better fire his ass before he gets himself killed."

"You got that right." Sully slowly shook his head.

"Aw, hell." Rex got to his feet and reached for his cane. "I'm going to find Nate. This is crazy. That kid shouldn't be left to work on his own."

Rex had no more than taken a single step when he spotted Lainie and tipped his worn cowboy hat at her. "Little lady. If you'll excuse me?"

"Of course," she said.

Rex grumbled something under his breath as he took off in search of the acting foreman.

"So," Sully said. "I see you're finally home after your trip to town."

"Yes, I got back a little while ago. I've been helping Drew get settled in the cabin on the knoll."

Sully glanced at his wristwatch. "Looks like it's about time for dinner."

Yes, and if she didn't get inside quickly, she wouldn't have it on the table by five o'clock. Joy had warned her that the men were in the habit of eating at set times— and not one minute later.

"I know you're probably busy," Sully said, "but I thought about something after we discussed your friend's problem."

For a moment, the only problem Lainie could remember was her own. What normal woman dropped her pants in front of a stranger, and all because of a tiny mouse? But Sully hadn't been privy to that secret. At least, not yet.

"What problem is that?" she asked.

"You know," he said, as he got up from his rocker and followed her into the kitchen. "The friend who wrote you the letter about having her heart broken."

"Oh, yes."

"I thought about something else you can tell her," Sully said.

Too late. The column was already in Mr. Carlton's inbox. But Lainie wasn't about to turn down any sage advice she might be able to use later. "What's that?"

"You can't expect someone else to make you happy. You'll only end up miserable if you do because the time will come when the two of you will part ways, through death or divorce or whatever."

Wasn't that the truth? Time and again since childhood, Lainie had learned that lesson the hard way. She never knew her mother, and her father died before she and her twin entered kindergarten. Three years later, her grandmother followed suit and left them wards of the state. Then Erica was adopted and snatched away. Even while Lainie was in the hospital for her heart surgery, the nurses kept changing, thanks to their varied shifts.

So if there was anything to count on, it was that life was unpredictable. And the only one who could make her happy was herself.

She'd thought her luck might have changed when

she met Craig, but she'd never expected him to make her *happy*. She had, however, expected him to be honest with her.

"When my wife died," Sully said, "I missed her so much. For a while, I thought my life was over. I couldn't see a purpose for it after she was gone. But my buddies stepped in and gave me a kick in the backside. They told me to quit feeling sorry for myself and to focus on others."

Lainie opened the commercial-sized refrigerator and pulled out a huge package of ground beef. "What did you do?"

"I volunteered at a local soup kitchen. And it made all the difference in the world. Tell your friend to find something to do that's bigger than herself. Once she gets off the pity train, she'll be surprised at how good she'll feel."

"More wise advice," Lainie said. And more fodder for a future column.

"You might want to give her some options, like volunteering at the animal shelter or collecting blankets and toiletry items for the homeless."

Actually, that's exactly what Lainie would so. She'd go to the library and do some online research about the needs in the community. Then, when she found an opportunity to make a suggestion like that to someone, she'd have a good-size list of volunteer possibilities to provide as a wrap to the column.

"That's a great idea, Sully. I'll make that suggestion the next time I talk to my friend." She offered him a warm, appreciative smile, dropped the meat on the counter then opened the pantry and pulled out several packages of buns. "Thanks again for the advice."

"Sure. Anytime. Say, you need any help?"

Boy, did she. And on so many levels. But he was talking about dinner—and the need for her to get it on the table by five. "Sure, would you mind firing up the gas grill?"

"I'd be delighted." Sully went outside to the deck.

Before forming the meat into patties, Lainie washed her hands at the sink, then dried them with the dish towel that had been resting on the counter. She couldn't help glancing out the kitchen window at the cabin on the knoll. Her hand lifted, and she fingered the length of the scar that hid under the cotton and denim.

She'd just about reached her wit's end when it came to dealing with handsome men, especially those who left her feeling guilty or embarrassed or lacking in any way. Fortunately, she'd be moving on again soon. Only this time, when she chose a new job, it might be best to consider one at a convent.

Lainie had just finished wiping down the countertops and putting away the last of the breakfast dishes when the ranch telephone rang. She snatched the receiver from its wall-mounted cradle. The cord, stretched from years of use, dangled to her knees. "Rocking Chair Ranch. This is Lainie."

"Hey, kid."

She was more than a little surprised to hear Mr. Carlton's voice on the other end.

"I knew you could do it," he said, his tone almost

jubilant. "That column you sent to me yesterday was great. In fact, it was everything I'd hoped it would be."

Thank goodness. Or rather, in this case, thank *Sully*. Either way, she was relieved to know she'd hit the mark. "Thank you, Mr. Carlton."

"You mentioned the internet service wasn't very good at the ranch, so I hope you received the additional letters I sent. I hadn't gotten your column yet, but I had a good feeling."

"Yes, I did. I had to go into town to find Wi-Fi so I could send it to you. And while I was there, I checked my email and downloaded them onto my laptop." She hadn't looked at them yet. She was waiting until she found both the time and the enthusiasm to tackle the chore. But her boss didn't need to know that. "I'll read them over the weekend."

"Good, but you might want to get started on them right away. I'll need your next column turned in by Monday at noon."

"So *soon*?" Monday was only a few days away. She leaned against the wall and wrapped the curly phone cord around her index finger. "I thought my deadlines were on Wednesdays."

"Now that we're back on track, I'll need more time to review your column."

"I'm afraid I'm not following you."

"When the last Dear Debbie quit without notice, I had to find a replacement and make adjustments. The column comes out every Friday, so I pushed your deadline back to give you time to write it. But that meant I had to review it quickly. I'll admit that your column isn't a huge priority to me, especially since the reader-ship isn't that big. But the fans we do have are very loyal. And they're vocal."

Lainie didn't doubt that the lovelorn column was at the bottom of the editor's priority list. Not that she knew what was at the top. She had no idea what the Brighton Valley residents expected to see in terms of news and special interest stories. At least, not yet. She'd have a much better idea after she researched her new community and the various organizations needing vol-unteers the next time she went to town. She'd even take her camera with her. Who knew what photo op she might find? Or what interesting tidbit she might learn. There were sure to be plenty of people or ac-tivities going on that she could use for a future article.

Mr. Carlton cleared his throat. "A Monday deadline isn't going to be a problem for you, is it?"

She'd wrapped the phone cord so tightly around her finger that it had turned red, so she loosened it as she attempted to reassure her boss. "No, not at all. I'll get my next column to you with time to spare." Now all she had to do was to reassure herself that she'd come through for him again.

And to pull that off, she'd have to find Sully. Maybe she could bribe him with brownies.

"That's just the kind of response I like in my staff," Mr. Carlton said. "My *full-time* staff."

He didn't have to say any more. If Lainie wanted a bigger and more important position at *The Brighton Valley Gazette*, she'd need to keep her self-doubt at bay.

"You won't be disappointed, Mr. Carlton."

"We'll see about that." He muttered something under his breath—or possibly to someone else. "Listen, Debbie—or rather, Lainie. I have a meeting and need to get ready for it. I'll let you go so you can get started on the next column. I can't wait to see it." Then he hung up without saying goodbye.

Lainie completely freed her finger from the cord, released her death grip on the receiver and returned it to the wall mount. Then she straightened her stance and blew out a ragged sigh.

She had plenty on her to-do list today, like cleaning out the refrigerator and mopping the kitchen floor. She hadn't considered her usual household tasks to be a burden until she thought about those darned letters, just waiting for a clever response.

She'd better read them now, while she ate her own breakfast. That way, she could ponder her answers while she worked.

After retrieving her laptop from her room, where it rested on the pine dresser, next to her prized high-definition camera, she returned to the kitchen. She wanted to be available in case the on-duty nurse or one of the men needed her, so couldn't very well hole up elsewhere.

She toasted a slice of sourdough bread. After smearing it with peanut butter, she poured a cup of coffee and seasoned it with cream and sugar. Then she took a seat at the table and got to work.

Twenty minutes later, she'd chosen a couple of interesting letters. One of them gave her a perfect opportunity to share Sully's advice about getting off the pity train and thinking about someone else for a change. But she was still at a loss when it came to providing any suggestions for the other. Sure, she always had an opinion. But what if she steered someone in the wrong direction? Or what if her words came out dull and uninteresting?

In spite of her best intentions, she couldn't seem to wake up her muse or stir her thoughts. So she went about her chores, racking her brain to come up with something to write.

Darn it. Could she do this again? Heck, she hadn't even done it last time without help.

Once the kitchen was spick-and-span, she sat at the table again, a fresh cup of coffee beside her laptop. She tried to focus on Mr. Carlton's praise, but even that wasn't enough to instill a burst of confidence.

That column you sent to me yesterday was great. It was everything I'd hoped it would be.

Maybe so, but Lainie hadn't done it on her own. She'd been stymied until Sully…

Yep. Sully.

She needed to find the retired cowboy and ask for more of his simple but sage advice. So where was he?

He'd gone outside for a walk after breakfast, but he could be back now. She closed her laptop, scooted her chair away from the table then got to her feet. She made her way to the sink and looked out the window in search of the man who might be able to help her keep her job at the *Gazette*.

Sully wasn't in the yard, but when her gaze drifted to the cabin on the knoll, she spotted another man. A much younger one who'd shed his fancy duds for worn jeans and a long-sleeved black T-shirt that molded to his muscular form.

Well, what do you know? Drew Madison might *appear* to be a country gentleman with the financial resources to hire others to do physical labor. Yet there he was, tearing apart the old porch as if he wasn't afraid to roll up his sleeves and get the job done himself.

Apparently, he'd gone to the hardware store earlier this morning because a pile of new lumber was stacked off to the side. But it wasn't the tools or the supplies that commanded her interest. It was the man in action.

Rugged and strong.

Masculine and focused.

Heat rushed her face, and her tummy went topsy-turvy. But her visceral reaction only served to send up a host of red flags and set off alarms in her head.

She couldn't trust herself when it came to choosing a man. Neither of the two who'd struck her fancy in the past had turned out to be honest, kind or worthy of her time and affection. Not a single one. So what made her think this guy was any different?

Instead of gawking at Drew, she studied him carefully, trying to spot the flaws he hid behind his Western wear or under his hat.

He was handsome, that was a fact. But handsome men, especially the last one, had done a real number on her in the past. She turned on the tap water and washed her hands as if that simple act might rid her of a silly attraction to a guy who'd probably broken more hearts than wild horses.

* * *

Drew tore a rotted piece of wood from the porch railing, then slung it to the pile he'd made off to the side. It felt good to work with his hands for a change. And he took a sense of pride in the fact that he was, in some small way, helping out the Rocking C Ranch. Better than tackling that blog.

As he swung his hammer to break away the last stretch of porch railing, he got a weird feeling in his core, a second sense that suggested someone was watching him. Instinctively, he turned around.

At first, he didn't see anyone. But then he looked at the house, where a feminine shape stood at the kitchen window.

It had to be Lainie. Who else could it be?

Then she disappeared from sight.

Had he caught her watching him? Or had she merely glanced out the window in passing, a coincidence that he'd turned at just the right time to find her there?

"Whatever," he muttered, gripping the hammer tighter. It was hard to say for sure. Besides, it didn't really matter. He had work to do, and now that he'd built up a sweat, he wanted to finish. He kicked a rotting board out of the way, just as a familiar voice of one of the retirees called out to him.

"Hey, you. College boy. What's going on?"

Drew turned from his work and spotted Rex Mayberry, his late granddad's old friend, limping toward him, using a cane. He wore a tattered hat over his bald head, and a wooden matchstick wiggled in the corner of his mouth. Just the sight of him was enough to draw a smile.

"I'm just trying to pay for my keep." Drew lifted his left arm and wiped the sweat from his brow with a sleeve. "How 'bout you? Feeling okay today?"

"As long as you don't count bad knees, crappy vision and dentures, I'm doing just hunky-dory." With his wry, crotchety sense of humor, Rex was the kind of man who didn't usually say much. But when he did, people gave him their full attention.

At least, Drew always had. He'd been about six years old and living on his grandfather's ranch the first time they'd met. It hadn't taken him long to respect the wisdom behind the man's words. But it wasn't just his comments that had been notable. Rex had been a damn good cowboy, one of the best. So it was tough to see him now, stooped and gray.

Rex let out a chuckle. "I'll bet that rich, candy-ass uncle of yours would be pissed if he saw you now."

Drew smiled. "Yep, you've got that right. J.P. doesn't think much about cowboys, rodeos or ranching. But what he doesn't know won't hurt him."

"I'm sure as hell not gonna tell him. Not after him and me had words after your high school graduation."

Drew hooked his thumbs into his back pockets and frowned. "I wasn't aware of that."

"Yeah, well, I figured your granddad would have wanted me to speak up on his behalf. So I did."

"What'd you say?"

"I told him that you were one of the best horsemen I'd ever seen. And that you were a born rancher. You would've turned the Double M around—if you'd had the chance—and then you would have been able to keep it in the family."

"I might have. If Uncle J.P. would have loaned us the money to pay the back taxes." Drew had only been eleven when his grandfather died, so there hadn't been much he could do to keep the ranch going. His mother had inherited the Double M, but she hadn't been able to make a go of it, especially after her cancer diagnosis. But that had been her secret until her health deteriorated to a certain point.

"I thought it was lousy of J.P. to offer his help, but only if he could call all the shots."

Drew had hoped his great-uncle would loan them the money to pay the back taxes, but J.P. had refused, saying he hadn't reached financial success by squandering his holdings.

Andrew, J.P. had said at the time, *you have a hell of a lot more going for you than being a cowboy. And you're too smart to risk your neck at a foolhardy way of life. So I'll tell you what I'm going to do. I'll pay for your college tuition, which is an investment in you— and in your future.*

"It was probably just as well," Drew said. "My mom had been in remission, but about that time, she got word that the cancer had come back. So J.P. told her to sell the ranch and move to the city with Kara Lee. Mom had access to better medical care there. And selling the ranch provided her with the money to pay for it."

Rex chuffed. "I know it was probably the right thing

to do for her, but I'm not so sure about your sister. She had a hard time changing high schools."

Neither of them mentioned the fact that Drew's mom had died anyway, leaving Kara Lee in Drew's care until she graduated.

"And what about you?" Rex asked. "You gave up your boyhood dreams at the request of your uncle."

"Yes, but not completely. I'm still a cowboy at heart."

And so was the old man leaning on his cane.

"Hold on," Drew said. "I'll bring out a chair for you. That way, you can watch what I'm doing. I'd hate for you to think I'm too book smart for my own good."

"Sure, I'll sit here for a spell. And just for the record, I never had much use for a man who thought he was too good to get his hands dirty or work up a good lather."

"Yes, I know."

"Your grandfather and me, we were cut from the same bolt of cloth. We thought a hard day's work and good deeds never hurt anyone. No, sir."

"I might work indoors most of the time," Drew said, "but I haven't forgotten any of the lessons you guys taught me."

"I'm glad to hear that. I was afraid those college professors would ruin you." Rex lifted his worn felt cowboy hat and raked his gnarled fingers through what was left of his graying hair. "Now get me that chair."

Drew winked at his old friend and mentor before climbing onto the porch. He entered the cabin and returned with one of two chairs from the small dinette table. He placed it in a shady spot.

The old man took a seat and leaned the cane against his knee. "I still think you could have been a champion bronc rider if you'd continued on the circuit."

"Maybe so. But under the circumstances, I don't have any major regrets. I have a good career with Esteban Enterprises. And someday soon, I'm going to create my own company, Silver Buckle Promotions."

"That's one heck of a name. I like it."

"Yep. I'm putting my education to good use. Besides, I still work in the rodeo world, only now I'm a promoter."

Drew had just turned back to his work when Rex asked, "So what's this I hear about you interviewing us? Are you writing an article for the newspaper?"

"No, I'm going to write a blog."

Rex let out a humph. "I'm not sure what that is, but I hope it'll help keep this ranch afloat."

Drew tore up a piece of the floorboard and tossed it on top of the pile of old wood. "That's just one part of the plan. And you'd better believe I'll give it my all." He wasn't so sure about the blog, but he knew he'd do a good job with the rest of the promotion. The Rocking C provided the old cowboys with an affordable and familiar place to live out their last years. So it was too important not to help them get the financial support they needed.

"That's good to know because I like it here—especially the food. That Joy is one fine cook. I was afraid that her temporary replacement wouldn't be worth a darn, but she's actually doing okay. What's her name? Lonnie? Lindy?"

"Lainie."

Rex nodded. "Yeah, well, she's been holding her own so far."

Drew glanced toward the house. When he didn't spot Lainie standing at the window, a pang of disappointment struck. But he shook it off. He wasn't here for fun and games. He had work to do.

Only problem was, he hadn't planned on meeting Lainie. Nor had he expected to get a glimpse of her wearing a pair of sexy panties. As the memory replayed in his mind, a smile spread across his face.

"She's a pretty one," Rex said.

Drew peeled his gaze away from the empty kitchen window and turned to his old friend. "I'm not sure I'm following you."

"The hell, you say." Rex laughed and pointed his thumb at the house. "Kid, I've always been able to read your face like a book."

That might have been true when Drew was a kid, but he'd learned to mask his expressions over the years. That is, unless he was caught off guard.

To throw Rex off course, he reached for the first excuse he could concoct. "I'm getting hungry and wondered if lunch was ready."

"Don't lie to me. The food won't be on the table 'til noon. And I watched you pack it away at breakfast. You might be working hard, kid, but not enough to want lunch at ten o'clock."

Okay, so he'd been caught. "If you haven't noticed, I've been working my tail off here."

"Yeah, right." Rex chuckled.

Rather than let the conversation continue, Drew turned back to demolish the rest of the porch. He wasn't going to give Rex further reason to connect romantic dots that weren't there.

Only trouble was, Drew couldn't help but wonder if there actually might be a few dots that could use a little connecting.

Chapter Four

Lainie had no sooner whipped up a batch of corn bread to go with the chili simmering on the stove, when Sully entered the house through the mudroom, whistling a spunky tune.

"Hey," she said, as she continued to pour the batter into the large, rectangular pan. "You're just the guy I was looking for. Where've you been?"

"Me?" He furrowed his bushy white brow. "I was out taking a morning walk. Then Nate asked me if I wanted to ride into town with him. What's up?"

"Not much. I talked to my friend and shared your advice with her. She realized you were right about the jerk she'd been dating. But then she told me about another friend of ours with a problem, and we're at odds on what to tell her."

Sully pulled out a chair and took a seat at the table. "So what's troubling that gal?"

"She's been saving her money for nearly a year and has enough to purchase a used car, which she desperately needs. Her old one keeps breaking down, and the repairs have been costly. On the upside, she now has a new, better-paying job. She needs dependable transportation, but her kid brother wants to borrow a thousand dollars to cover his rent and the late fee."

Sully rested his clasped hands on the table and steepled his fingers. "Can she spare the money?"

"Yes, if she doesn't buy the car." Lainie placed the pan into the prewarmed oven and set the timer. "Her brother promised to repay her next month, but to complicate matters, he hasn't always repaid the loans she's given him in the past."

"Sounds like she has every reason to turn him down this time."

"I think so, too, but she's been taking care of him ever since their parents died." Lainie could certainly relate to the woman's love and compassion. If she and her twin hadn't been separated, she'd feel the same sense of responsibility.

"How old is the boy?"

"He's twenty-four now and living on his own. But she's worried about him getting evicted, especially since he can't seem to keep a job."

"Apparently, he hasn't had to. His sister keeps jumping in to save the day."

"She means well," Lainie said.

"Yes, but by bailing him out every time he gets into

a jam, she's robbing him of the ability to learn from his mistakes."

Wow. That was an interesting way to look at it. And wise, too.

"Listen," Sully said. "If her no-account brother can't come up with the money to cover his rent this month, how is he going to pay it next month and also be able to repay her as promised?"

"Good point."

"Your friend is allowing her heart to get in the way of her brains. Her brother might have one sob story after another, but it's time for him to grow up. And it's time for his sister to let him."

"You're absolutely right. Thanks." Lainie could work with that sound advice. She'd just have to put her own spin on it.

The back door squeaked open. When she glanced up, she spotted Drew entering the kitchen. His hair was damp and freshly combed, suggesting that he'd recently showered. He'd changed clothes, too.

White button-down shirt. Clean jeans. Shiny cowboy boots.

Their eyes met, and Lainie found it impossible to look away.

He closed the gap between them, and she caught an alluring whiff of masculine soap. Her breath caught, and her voice squeaked out a greeting. "Hey, Drew."

He responded with a "Hey" of his own, his deep voice rumbling through her. She wasn't sure she'd be able to conjure a response until Sully cleared his throat, drawing Lainie's attention away from the handsome man who stood a mere arm's length away.

"If you two will excuse me," Sully said. "I'm going to rest up before the noon meal." Then he shuffled out of the room.

"Something sure smells good," Drew said.

He clearly meant the food, but by the way his gaze caressed her, she wasn't sure. Nevertheless, she couldn't very well stand here like a ditz. So she gathered her wits and said, "I saw you earlier when I glanced out the window and into the yard. I thought you were only going to fix a couple of steps. I had no idea you were going to replace the porch."

"The whole thing was shot. I wasn't going to nail new lumber to bad."

"That makes sense." But what didn't make sense was the way her pulse was racing. Or the way he was looking at her right now. It seemed as if he could see right into her heart.

She touched her throat to check the top button on her flannel shirt before trailing her fingers along the soft blue fabric that covered her chest. When she reached the waistline of her jeans, she realized what she'd been doing and placed her hands on her hips.

He grinned.

And why wouldn't he? He probably thought she was flirting with him, that she had something romantic on her mind, but she didn't. Well, maybe just a little, but she wouldn't allow her curiosity and sexual awareness to get the better of her.

"No overalls today?" he asked, arching a single brow.

"They're in the laundry. I have two pairs, actually. But I don't always wear them. I like them, though. I got them on sale at the local feed store. Very utilitarian. You know?"

She nearly winced at her response. Could she sound any more ditzy or moonstruck?

He nodded, his gaze again scanning her from the topknot on her head to her shoes, then back again. Her toes curled inside her sneakers, causing her to sway. Oh, for Pete's sake. She had to put a stop to the girlishness. She was practically swooning.

Back to business. She turned to the counter, picked up a spoon and started stirring the chili in the pot.

"So when will you finish those repairs?" she asked, her back to him.

"I tore apart the old porch and hauled off all the bad wood. I'll start on the new carpentry tomorrow."

"That'll make entering the front door a little awkward. It's a big step."

"Not for me."

No, she supposed it wouldn't be. The man had to be six feet tall or more. Looking at his handsome face was hard enough. But when he spoke with a faint Southern drawl, his voice had a lulling effect on her.

She placed the spoon on a plate, stepped away from the stove, then brushed her hands on her denim-clad hips, as if her jeans had somehow gotten dusty.

Oh, my gosh. Stop fidgeting and get it together, Lainie.

She offered him her best attempt at an unaffected smile and changed the subject yet again. "I hope you like chili beans and corn bread because that's on the menu for lunch."

"It sounds good."

Her face heated. She hadn't meant to tell him something he could figure out for himself by looking at the stove, but the man was too distracting.

"I was going to interview one of the retired cowboys before we eat," he said. "But now that I've caught a mouthwatering aroma of what's to come, I'd rather hang out in here. Is there anything I can do to help you?" He nodded toward the cupboard. "I'd be happy to set the tables."

"Sure, thanks."

Nate and the young ranch hands usually ate in the kitchen. The retirees were served in the dining room. But he'd know that from being there for several meals, so there was no need to offer further instruction.

Off he went with the plates into the dining room. Moments later he returned for the silverware.

As he moved about the kitchen, close enough to bump into her, close enough for her to catch his musky scent, it was difficult to think, let alone respond to any friendly chatter.

She ought to be thankful for his help, but the only thing that would truly help her right now would be for him to go in search of one of the cowboys, like he'd planned to do.

"I can finish up," she told him. "Why don't you round up someone to interview before lunch?"

And take your sexy smile, hunky self and mesmerizing scent with you.

Drew didn't know why he'd insisted on helping Lainie in the kitchen. As a kid, he'd resented doing what he'd considered women's work. But later, after his mother started chemo and was sick more often than not, he'd taken on meal preparation for their family of three. That included the planning, shopping and cooking. So he'd gained a new respect for cooks—male or female.

But that still didn't explain why he'd stepped up and was now counting out mismatched flatware from the drawer. Lainie was certainly capable of handling things on her own.

The fact that he found her attractive was undoubtedly a contributing factor. And if anything, the more time he spent with her, the more appealing he found her to be.

She didn't wear makeup, which gave her a wholesome, girl-next-door look, which he found alluring. Hot, even. And her faint floral scent? It was enough to make a man perk up and take notice of her every move.

She rocked those baggy jeans and that oversize T-shirt like an urban model, the kind that didn't give a damn about what other people thought. And she pulled it off right down to her sneakers.

Once again his mind drifted to the mouse encounter, when he'd gotten a peek at her shapely legs and those sexy panties, and he'd begun to see her in a whole new light. An arousing one.

He found the contradiction, the soft femininity of silk and lace hidden behind durable denim, to be incredibly sensual. It not only spiked his testosterone, it piqued his curiosity. And that, he decided, was what prompted him to offer his help today.

After he finished setting both tables, he returned to the kitchen, pausing just inside the doorway to watch Lainie work. Her back was to him, so she was unaware that he'd stolen the opportunity to study her.

She snatched a potholder from the counter, then opened the oven door, withdrew the corn bread and placed it on one side of the stovetop to cool. Next she checked the chili beans simmering in a pot.

Rather than continue to admire her, Drew said, "I finished setting the table. Is there anything else I can do?"

She turned to face him, her cheeks flushed a deeper shade of pink. She touched her collar, fiddling with the top button. When she caught his eye, her hand dropped to her side.

"You can fill the glasses with ice." She nodded to the countertop, where two large gallon jars held tea. "Most of the men like to have sweet tea with all their meals."

"Consider it done."

As Drew made his way toward the cupboard and near Lainie, she bit down on her bottom lip. "Don't get me wrong. I appreciate this, but I'm not used to having help."

"It's no problem."

She offered him a waifish smile. Something in those expressive brown eyes suggested that she'd been on her own for a while. And that it hadn't been by her own choosing.

He pulled glasses from the cupboard. "You mentioned having a twin—and that you hadn't seen her in a while."

When Lainie didn't immediately respond, he realized that he'd overstepped. He didn't have the right to pry or to ask about the dynamics of her family, but for some reason, his curiosity grew too strong to ignore.

"I take it you and your sister aren't very close," he said, prodding her.

"We used to be." Her voice came out soft, fragile, stirring his sympathy along with his interest.

"Did you have a falling-out?" he asked.

She paused for the longest time, and he just stood there, a glass in hand, waiting while the moment turned awkward.

He was about to apologize for getting too personal when she said, "Her name is Erica, but I called her Rickie. We haven't seen each other since we were nine and she was adopted."

Wow. Drew hadn't seen that coming.

"Were you adopted, too?" he asked.

"No, I...remained in foster care."

The waning sense of awkwardness rose up again, stronger than ever. Under any other circumstances, he might have turned away, changed the subject. Yet he felt compelled to dig for more information, even though each time she answered one of his questions, it only served to trigger another.

"Have you considered looking for her?" he asked. "I mean, now that you're adults."

"I think about that all the time, but it was a closed adoption, so there's not much I can do."

"Feel free to tell me to mind my own business, but why didn't her parents adopt you, too?"

"It's complicated." She reached for her collar again. A nervous habit, he supposed. "We were both living in foster care at the time. I… Well, I had a few health problems back then and was moved to a home with better access to medical care. While I was gone, a family came along and chose her, but not me."

"I'm sorry." That must have hurt like hell.

"Don't be. I was sad, but I understood why. I've dealt with it."

"Have you?"

"I just said I had."

"I mean, most kids would have felt hurt, left out, rejected. Some might even carry those feelings for years."

"Not me. Don't worry about it."

"I'm sorry if I stirred up any sad memories."

She shrugged. "Like I said, I've dealt with it." Then she turned her back to him and returned to her work, ending a conversation that had gotten way too personal and revealing for his own good.

Yet for some crazy reason, he was tempted to embrace her, to press her head to his shoulder and tell her he sympathized with her over the rejection and the loss of her sister. But he didn't.

He might be a sucker for innocent, vulnerable women, but he wasn't about to take on another one now. Not when he had his plate full with a pregnant sister on bed rest.

"How about you?" Lainie asked. "Do you have any siblings?"

"Yes, a kid sister." And she was the only family he had left. Well, so far. "She's expecting a baby boy at the end of March."

"That's nice. Uncle Drew, huh?"

He grinned. "That's right."

"I take it you're close."

"Yeah, we're pretty tight." At Kara Lee's wedding, Drew had been the one to give her away. Then he'd stood back, his head held high, a smile on his face.

He'd been glad to know that she'd finally grown up, that she'd have a home and family of her own. That she'd have the happiness she'd always deserved. He'd assumed that Craig was an honorable man. That he'd step up and take care of Kara Lee from that day on, for richer or poorer, in sickness and in health.

But that wasn't to be. And it hadn't been death that parted them, but a parade of lovers. The last straw was the sexy brunette whose video had gone viral.

A woman who hadn't had any more respect for sacred wedding vows than Craig Baxter had.

While Lainie tidied up the kitchen after the evening meal, Drew and one of the retired cowboys remained at the table, having a cup of decaf.

Drew had set up a small video recorder, a real nice one. The kind that, if Lainie hit the lottery, she'd buy.

"Damn it. I can't get this thing to record."

Lainie had planned to stay in the background, but she couldn't help going to the rescue. "Here. You have it on the wrong mode. That's all." She triggered the right one. "There you go."

The elderly cowboy, Gilbert Henry, laughed. "Guess you're an old soul like me, Drew. Can't figure out that newfangled equipment."

"Something like that."

Lainie scrubbed a counter that didn't need cleaning and listened to Gilbert talk about his time in the Marine Corps during the Korean War, his return to the States and his marriage to Pearl, his high school sweetheart.

"We bought a house in Wexler," Gil said. "We had dreams, me and Pearl. She wanted a big family, and I was prepared to give that little gal anything she wanted. But I guess God or Fate had other plans. We tried to have a baby for nearly ten years. Finally, we adopted two little boys—brothers who'd been orphaned at a young age."

Lainie couldn't help but wish that a couple like Gil and his wife had been around when she and Rickie needed a home.

"Ray was the oldest," Gil said. "And was he a real pistol. Sharp as a tack, but never did like school. Jimmy was the youngest. And quiet. For a while, we never thought he'd ever say a word. But once he did, he jabbered from morning until night."

"Where are they now?" Drew asked.

"When Ray was sixteen, he got caught up with the wrong crowd and ended up on drugs." Gil clucked his tongue. "And he got sent to the state pen for a while, too. Damn near broke Pearl's heart and caused a divorce when I refused to bail him out. But hell, he was going to have to serve time anyway and I didn't trust him to show up in court."

"That must have been very hard on you and your wife."

"Yep. But in the long run, Ray's incarceration turned out to be a blessing. Thanks to a prison ministry, he turned his life around. Believe it or not, he's a preacher in Louisiana. He doesn't have a big fancy church. He spends a lot of his time on the street corner, passing out Bibles and giving sandwiches to the homeless. But he seems to be happy doing that."

"How about the younger boy?" Drew asked.

"We lost him in Desert Storm."

Lainie stopped scrubbing and looked over her shoulder at the man.

Gil's voice cracked. "I keep his Silver Star on my nightstand to remember him by."

"I'm sorry to hear that," Drew said.

"Me, too. But you should have seen the letters some of his buddies sent to us and the articles written in the paper. I'm damn proud to know I raised a boy who didn't balk when it came to dying to save the men in his platoon."

Lainie had already tidied up the kitchen, but rather than leave the men alone, she began reorganizing the pantry, which really didn't need it. Joy kept an organized kitchen. She also kept two bottles of wine in there and had told Lainie she was welcome to open either or both. But Lainie wouldn't do that.

She shuffled some of the canned goods, wasting time so she could continue to eavesdrop and hear what Gilbert had to say. But after mentioning Pearl's death two years ago, just days after their sixtieth wedding anniversary, the interview stalled.

"Well," Gil said, as he got up from his seat. "I guess that's pretty much all I have to say."

"Thanks for your candor and your time," Drew told him.

Lainie watched Gil shuffle from the room, her heart heavy with the bittersweet memories he'd shared. She knew each of the retirees at the Rocking C had unique backgrounds, filled with both sad and happy times, but hearing Gil's story reminded her that they weren't forgotten stories.

Drew shut off the video recorder and blew out a ragged breath. "Writing this blog is going to be even more difficult than I thought it'd be."

"Because of Gil's interview?"

"Yes. You were in here and heard his story. My heart goes out to that guy. His life seems pretty tragic, and I'm not sure how to go about writing it."

Lainie closed the pantry door, turned to face Drew and leaned against the kitchen cupboard. "All you have to do is put the right spin on it. You can choose to portray Gil as a tired, grieving old man. Or you can show him as a loving husband and proud father who raised sons who have made this world a better place."

"Good point. The older boy spent time in prison, but he learned from his mistakes."

"And the younger brother made the ultimate sacrifice for his country."

"Yeah. Gil and his wife were good parents, whose sons have sacrificed for others. I'm not sure if I can do them all justice."

"Sure you can. Follow your heart, and you'll do right by them."

He stared at his notes and frowned. "But I don't even know where to begin."

"I could help out. I have a degree in journalism." Shoot. Why had she made an offer like that?

"No kidding?"

She crossed her arms and shifted her weight to one hip. "Don't look so surprised. This job at the ranch is only temporary. And while it's come in handy for the time being, I'm going to work at a newspaper someday."

Actually, she was working for one now, but that was her secret. Besides, writing the Dear Debbie column certainly didn't make her an investigative reporter or a photojournalist.

A grin stretched across Drew's face, lighting his eyes. "I'm impressed. I don't suppose I could hire you to give me some editorial direction for that blog? Would you be up for that?"

Did he mean to pay her for her time? She was going to offer her services for free, but she could sure use the additional income. "You want to hire me?"

"Absolutely. I'm not sure what the going rate is, but I'll gladly pay it."

Lainie tempered her enthusiasm and said, "Sure. I'd be glad to help. Besides, it's for a good cause."

"It certainly is. I'd hate to see this place close."

"Me, too. The men seem happy here, even when they complain about the competency of some of the young ranch hands."

He laughed. "Sully calls them 'whippersnappers.'"

Lainie had heard plenty of comments from all the men. And she'd watched out the kitchen window one day when a couple of them, using a cane and a walker, approached the corral and gave one of the young hands a scolding for doing things wrong. It was a real sight. She'd wished she'd had her camera handy.

"You know," Lainie said, "I also have a minor in photography."

"No wonder you knew how to work my video recorder. Do you have a camera?"

"Yes. And I can take pictures of the ranch and the men to go along with your blog."

"That'd be great. We can show the young cowboys at work, as well as the old guys."

Lainie had a feeling she was going to like collaborating with Drew on the blog project. She might not have the perfect job at the *Gazette* yet, but at least she could get some more experience on her resume.

"I feel like celebrating," he said. "Too bad we don't have any champagne handy."

Toasting with crystal flutes and drinking sparkling wine with a handsome rodeo promoter sounded tempting. And while she knew where Joy's wine was, she wasn't about to lower her guard around a man like him. She'd been attracted to two other men in her life, and both had proven to be lacking in character.

And now here was another. Would the third time be the charm? Or another disaster?

Either way, she'd need to keep her wits about her.

"I have cookies and milk," she said in her best kindergarten teacher's voice.

"Then that'll have to do." Drew tossed her a dazzling smile, his eyes sparkling like fine champagne.

Yes, it would have to. Lainie removed several snickerdoodles from an airtight plastic container in the pantry and placed them on a plate. Then she poured them each a glass of milk.

All the while, Drew watched her. His gaze intensified, as if he knew that she wore white lace lingerie under her clothes, the one feminine luxury she'd refused to give up during the last reinvention of herself.

He reached for a cookie. "I'm looking forward to putting our heads together on the blog."

The thought of their heads touching, their breaths mingling...

Oh, for Pete's sake, Lainie. What were you thinking?

She took a sip of milk in an attempt to shake the inappropriate thought, but when she stole a peek at him and spotted his boyish grin, it didn't work. Images of romantic scenes continued to hound her.

She should have known better than to offer to help him with that stupid blog. With her luck, the assignment would end up being more trouble than it was worth.

So she did her best to shake off his mesmerizing gaze and her heart-stirring reaction to it by stuffing a cookie into her mouth.

Like it or not, she was stuck working closely with the gorgeous cowboy, and she'd just have to keep her growing attraction to him in check. Or she'd have to stuff herself with more milk and cookies.

Chapter Five

Over the next few days, while Lainie washed the dinner dishes, Drew conducted his first interviews in the kitchen.

"Since you offered to help me write that blog, or however many stories we have to tell," he'd told her, "you should hear what the men have to say."

Lainie agreed. And it certainly wasn't a hardship. The retired cowboys' memories and reflections were both touching and entertaining.

But their stories weren't the only thing that held her interest each evening. Drew's voice had a mesmerizing effect on her, and in spite of her efforts to ignore his soft Southern drawl, she found herself increasingly drawn to the rodeo promoter.

She was also touched by the kindness and respect

he'd shown the old guys, which made her think he might be different from the men who'd let her down in the past. Clearly, her first impressions of him hadn't been on target.

After placing a meat loaf in the top oven and the russet potatoes in the bottom, she washed her hands at the sink and peered out the window at his cabin, which now had a new front porch.

Drew wasn't anywhere in sight, so she leaned to the right and arched her neck to get a better view of the barn and yard. She still didn't see him, but she spotted Nate working with a fidgety colt in the corral. She'd heard about the acting foreman's skill with horses, but to see him in action was an amazing sight.

She'd already taken a number of shots of the cowboys, old and young alike, and this was a perfect opportunity to get another. She shut off the faucet, dried her hands on a dish towel and hurried to get her camera.

Moments later, she opened the mudroom door and stepped into the yard, her camera lens raised.

"Good job," a familiar, mesmerizing voice called out. "I'm glad to see you're taking advantage of a photo op."

Lainie didn't have to glance over her shoulder to see Drew's approach, but she turned to him anyway.

He looked good today in that black hat cocked just right and that chambray shirt, pressed with a dash of starch—thanks to a laundry service, no doubt. And those jeans? He wore them as if they were a part of him.

As he closed in on her, his scent—something alluring, manly and no doubt expensive—stirred her senses.

Her heart rate soared, and her arm wobbled, nearly causing her to drop her camera.

Oh, for Pete's sake. Get it together, girl.

Determined to shake off the effect Drew had on her, she nodded toward the corral. "The men told me that Nate was the resident horse whisperer, so I thought I'd get a couple pictures of him for the blog."

"Good idea." Drew offered her a heart-strumming smile and followed it up with a playful wink that would tempt the most diligent female employee to play hooky from work. "I'd better not interrupt you."

He had that right. She had a job to do, a photo to take. So she adjusted the lens and checked the light. After catching several shots of Nate, she lowered the camera to her side and focused on Drew. "I missed seeing you this morning. Where'd you run off to?"

"I met a friend for breakfast at Caroline's Diner."

She wondered if his friend was male or female, but decided it would be rude to come right out and ask. However, that didn't mean she couldn't prod him for a little more information.

"From what I saw, it seems that Caroline's is the place where all the locals eat. The food is good, and the desserts are amazing," she said. "Don't you think?"

"That's for sure." He splayed a hand on his flat belly and grinned. "But I'd better not make a habit of filling up on her hotcakes and maple syrup."

Maybe not, but he still hadn't given Lainie a clue about who he'd met, so she pumped a little more. "You and your friend must've had a lot of catching up to do. It's nearly lunchtime."

"Before heading back to the ranch, I stopped by the hardware store to buy more lumber. My cabin isn't the only one with a rickety, worn-out porch."

"You mean you're going to fix each one?"

"I might." He lifted his hat long enough to rake a hand through his hair.

"That's a nice thing for you to do." It was also generous, which was yet another reason to believe he might be a man worth her time and affection.

Lainie lifted her camera to take a picture of him, but he waved her off, blocking his face with his hand.

"Cut that out," he said, his tone playful and light. "That blog isn't about me."

"Okay, cowboy." She lowered her lens, but her gaze lingered on him. She really ought to return to the house, but she couldn't seem to make a move in that direction.

The thump of her heartbeats counted out several seconds until footsteps sounded and she spotted Bradley Jamison approaching.

The young ranch hand cleared his throat. "Excuse me. I hate to interrupt."

It was probably best that he did. Lainie offered him a smile. "What's up?"

"Nate said I could use one of the cabins for a few days. I don't want to cause you any trouble, ma'am, so I'd be happy to clean it up, if it needs it."

Drew answered Brad before Lainie could. "I thought you slept in the bunkhouse. Is someone giving you a hard time in there?"

"Oh, no. The cabin's not for me. It's for my mom.

She just got hired to work at the new children's home down the road. Once she's on their payroll, she'll get room and board there, but she doesn't start until Monday, and her lease is up tomorrow. So it would only be a couple of days."

"The new *children's* home?" Lainie asked.

Brad nodded sagely. "It's a place for abused and neglected kids. A man and his wife bought the old Clancy place and opened it up last month."

"I know where that ranch is," Drew said. "It's got a big house, but it's pretty old. I doubt it's up to code."

"It wasn't at first. But last summer, the community church got involved with the project, and so did the Wexler Women's Club. The couple in charge are trying to get a grant of some kind, but in the meantime, they'll have to slowly add kids as they go."

Still stunned by the idea of a children's home down the road, Lainie asked, "How many kids live there?"

"I think about twelve. Most of them are from the city. My mom told me the idea was to move them to a country environment so they could see a new way of life."

"That's an interesting concept," Drew said.

"Yeah." Brad replaced his hat on his head. "My mom was pretty impressed when she went out and saw it for herself. From what I understand, each kid is given certain chores, and they're also assigned a few animals to take care of—like pigs, sheep, goats and rabbits."

Lainie hoped they didn't plan to work the children too hard. She'd had one set of foster parents who'd been awfully strict and expected more out of her than seemed fair.

"What's your mom's job going to be?" Drew asked.

"They hired her as a counselor. After she divorced my stepdad, she went back to school. It took a while because she had to work during the day and take classes at night, but she finally got a degree."

"Good for her." Lainie liked the woman already.

"Yeah, I'm proud of her." Brad kicked the toe of his boot at the ground, stirring the dirt. "She's glad she'll be there before Christmas. A lot of those kids never had a tree or presents before. Their funds are limited, though, so she can't go all out with decorations and stuff, but she doesn't think it'll take much to make them happy."

"Actually," Lainie said, "regular meals and a warm, safe place to sleep helps a lot." Of course, that wouldn't change the reality those kids lived with each day, the memories they carried. "Don't worry, Brad. I'll make sure the cabin is ready for your mom."

Drew placed his hand on Lainie's shoulder, giving it a gentle squeeze. "No, you don't have to do that. I'll do it for you. You never know, a mouse might be lying in wait."

Lainie's cheeks warmed. She was tempted to plant an elbow in his side and shoot him a frown. But in truth, he'd just offered to do her a huge favor.

"Thanks," Brad said. "I really appreciate this. And just so you know, my mom said she'd be happy to help out around here. She'll cook, clean, run errands…whatever. She'll even keep some of those pesky old cowboys out of your hair. She's good with people, even difficult ones."

"I'm looking forward to meeting her," Lainie said. "And I'm sure we'll keep her busy while she's here."

"Well, I'd best get back to work or Nate'll have my hide." Brad tilted the brim of his hat to Lainie, turned and strode toward the barn.

Rather than let the subject of their conversation drift back to that embarrassing mouse encounter, Lainie steered it in another direction. "I hadn't given Christmas much thought, but I really ought to put up some holiday decorations, including a tree."

"I'm going to my sister's house on Christmas Day, but the rest of the time I'll be on the ranch, so I can help you." Drew nodded toward a couple of older men rocking on the porch. "Imagine the memories Christmas must dig up for these guys."

True. More fodder for Drew's blog...and for another human interest column for her to propose to Mr. Carlton. She could see it now: *A Cowboy Christmas*.

As Lainie began making a mental list of the chores to be done, she had a lightbulb moment. "Oh, wow."

"What's wrong?"

"Nothing. I just had an idea. What if we have a joint Christmas party for the children here at the Rocking C?"

"That'd be nice, but it would be a huge undertaking."

"Maybe, but I'm sure Rex, Sully and the others would help. And it would give the men a special purpose, not to mention something to look forward to."

Drew looked out in the distance, his brow creased in

concentration. After a couple of beats, he brightened. "You know, a party like that would lend itself to one heck of a blog post."

"You read my mind." A grin slid across Lainie's face, and a tingle of excitement spread through her.

She couldn't remember the last time she'd looked forward to Christmas, but she'd do whatever she could to create a special holiday for those kids. Decorations, a tree, holiday baking…

"We can do this." Lainie clutched Drew's arm in camaraderie, but she nearly jerked away when the body heat radiating through his shirt sent an electrical zing through her.

She tried to blame the spark on the energy emanating from their new joint venture, although she feared it was more than that.

"I'll find out who's in charge of the children's home," Drew said. "And I'll see how they feel about joining us for a Christmas party at the Rocking Chair Ranch."

"And I'll talk to our nursing staff," Lainie said, "although I can't see why they'd object. A party would be good for young and old alike."

"There's only two weeks before Christmas, so we have our work cut out for us. We'd better get busy." Drew gave Lainie's shoulder a nudge with his arm, reminding her of his presence, of his heat. They'd become a team, and by the way he was looking at her, he liked that idea.

She liked it, too.

As Drew turned and walked away, she studied his

back, admiring his sexy swagger, his broad shoulders and the perfect fit of his jeans.

A romantic wish tingled through her, warming her cheeks once again. Maybe Santa would be good to her for a change.

And if she was lucky, she just might wake up on Christmas morning and find a cowboy under her tree.

Drew was always up for a challenge, which is why he'd searched every nook and cranny of his cabin to find a cell signal. He was determined to set up a temporary but functional home office, although he wasn't having much luck. About the time he considered giving up and driving to town for Wi-Fi, he picked up a signal near the kitchen area.

As long as he moved the dinette table about three feet from the east wall, he could connect to the internet, which would make it a lot easier to work while he stayed at the ranch for the next two weeks.

Once he set up his laptop and got online, he did some research on the children's home Brad had mentioned earlier this afternoon. It was called Kidville, and from the pictures posted on the main website page, the outside looked like a small town in the Old West.

"Interesting," he said, as he continued to read up on the place that had been founded by Jim and Donna Hoffman, an older couple who had a heart for kids.

The more Drew learned about the Hoffmans and Kidville, the more determined he was to meet with them and see it for himself. With the Wi-Fi service he now had, it didn't take him long to find the number for the administrative office and ask for whoever was in charge.

A couple minutes later, Mr. Hoffman answered. "This is Jim. How can I help you?"

Drew introduced himself and revealed his affiliation with Esteban Enterprises, the rodeo and the Rocking Chair Ranch, and his admiration for what the Hoffmans were doing.

"Thanks," Jim said. "For nearly ten years, my wife and I dreamed of creating a place in the country where we could provide a safe, loving environment for abused and neglected city kids. So when we retired from our county jobs, we set our plan in motion. We've had a few hurdles along the way, so Kidville has been nearly two years in the making."

"I'd imagine funding would be one of those problems."

"Yes, that's true. But thanks to the help of the community church, the Wexler Women's Club and the Brighton Valley Rotary, we were able to remodel the house and get it up to code, paint the barn and set up a playground. But until we get more financial backing, we're nearing our capacity."

"I think it would be fairly easy to drum up support for such a worthy cause." Drew went on to explain his promotional plan for the retired cowboys' home.

"As a nonprofit, I'm afraid we don't have the funds to pay for any advertisements or PR companies," Jim said.

Apparently, Drew hadn't made himself clear. "I didn't expect you to hire me or Esteban Enterprises.

To be completely candid, I'm not exactly sure what I can do to help you and Kidville, but just for the record, nothing tugs at my boss's heartstrings more than rodeos, aging cowboys and children."

Drew didn't mention anything about a Christmas party on the Rocking C, but he did suggest a meeting with the Hoffmans. He could propose the idea at that time.

"Why don't you come by Friday afternoon?" Jim suggested. "We'll talk more then, and I can give you a tour of Kidville."

"Sounds like a plan. And if it's okay with you, I'll probably bring my...um, associate. It was her idea to do some joint promotion, and there's no telling what we might come up with if we all put our heads together."

"I'll make sure my wife is available. Would two o'clock work for the two of you?"

"That's perfect. We'll see you then." After the call ended, Drew continued to sit at the dinette table, his cell phone in hand. He had a good feeling about Kidville. And he couldn't wait to share the news with Lainie.

He glanced at the clock on the microwave. It was closing in on five o'clock and would soon be time for dinner. If he'd learned one thing in his week spent on the Rocking C, it was that the meals ran on a strict schedule.

He wouldn't say anything about it at the table. Instead, he'd wait until after everyone ate, when it was quiet in the kitchen.

And when he had Lainie to himself.

* * *

Other than several murmurs of appreciation for a tasty meal, the men had eaten quietly, their focus on the meat loaf, buttered green beans and baked potatoes. Even Drew, who sat at the kitchen table with the young ranch hands, hadn't said much, but by the glimmer in his eyes and the grin on his face, he seemed to be pleased about something.

Lainie tamped down her curiosity for now. She'd wait until after dinner to question him.

In the meantime, while the men had ice cream and chocolate chip cookies for dessert, she carried the plates and flatware to the sink, rinsed them off and placed them in the dishwasher. By the time she returned to the table for the empty bowls and spoons, the ranch hands were already filing out the back door, with Drew in the midst of them.

Lainie continued her work, putting away leftovers and wiping down countertops, but she couldn't help wondering what Drew was up to. For the past few evenings, he'd interviewed the retired cowboys in the kitchen, a routine she'd come to look forward to.

She glanced out the kitchen window. The lights were off in his cabin, so he hadn't turned in for the night. She'd just placed the detergent in the dishwasher when the back door swung open and clicked shut. She turned to see Drew striding through the mudroom on his way back inside.

His smile, as dazzling as it'd ever been, lit his eyes, and her pulse rate kicked up a notch.

"Got a minute?" he asked.

"Sure. What's up?"

He pulled out a chair from the table for her. "I thought you might like an update."

She sat down, and he took a seat next to her. "I did a little research, and Kidville, that children's home, appears to be everything Brad said it was and more. So I made an appointment for us to take a tour on Friday at two. Can you slip off for an hour or so?"

"I'd really like to, but I'm not sure. I'm usually busy with the meal prep for dinner at that time."

"I've got you covered. Brad's mother will be here by then, and a few minutes ago, when I mentioned what I had in mind, he called her. She said she'd be happy to cook dinner—or do anything else to help out. She's coming to stay that day anyway, so she's going to arrive a few hours early. You'll have plenty of time to show her around the kitchen."

"You've thought of everything."

"I try to cover all my bases." His wink turned her heart inside out.

They'd not only become teammates, but it seemed as if they were well on the road to being friends.

She liked the thought of that.

"Did you know that Kidville has a small orchard and a good-size vegetable garden?" Drew asked. "They're going to grow most of their produce, and they're raising chickens."

A niggle of concern crept over her, stealing her smile. "I know the kids will have chores, but I hope they won't be expected to do all the work."

"Jim Hoffman and his wife believe children should

be given age-appropriate responsibilities, and I see the reasoning behind that."

"Me, too. I just hope this doesn't turn out to be a farm run by child labor." Lainie's thoughts drifted to the time she'd lived with the Bakers, the memory taking her back to a place and foster family she'd hoped to forget.

"You have a faraway look in your eyes," Drew said, drawing her back to the here and now.

"I'm sorry. My mind wandered for a moment."

"To a bad personal experience?"

Lainie didn't usually talk about her early years—at least, not in detail. But she'd grown close to Drew in the past few days, and if they'd truly become friends, she should be up front with him. "I told you that I grew up in foster care. For the most part it wasn't too bad. If I'd been able to stay with the first family…" Tears filled her eyes, and she blinked them away. So much for the candor of friendship.

"I'm sorry that you had such a crappy childhood," he said.

"It wasn't all bad." She swiped at her lower lashes, stopping the overflow. "Most of the families I lived with were decent. In fact, I actually liked Mama Kate, the first foster mother my sister and I had. She was an older, dark-skinned woman who had an easy laugh and a loving heart as big as her lap. She never turned down a kid needing a placement, so there were a lot of us. Yet she managed to find special time for each of us. My sister and I counted ourselves lucky to live with her."

"Why'd you have to leave?" Drew asked.

"One night, about six months after we moved in, Mama Kate had a stroke and had to give us all up."

"That's too bad. Where did you go next?"

Lainie bit back a quick response. She wasn't sure she wanted to be that up front. She and Rickie had moved to a receiving home, where her heart condition was finally diagnosed. She endured several back-to-back hospitalizations, which was when she and her sister were separated. After her surgery and a long inpatient recuperation period, she learned that Rickie had been adopted. Sadly, they'd never had a chance to say good-bye to each other.

But Lainie wasn't going to share that.

She reached for her collar, fingered the top button then skimmed the next three before dropping her hand to her lap. "Next stop was to the Bakers' house. Talk about all work and no play."

"So that's why you're worried about the children and their chores at Kidville," Drew said.

"The Bakers seemed to think that I was there to cook, clean the house and do the laundry."

"An unpaid servant, huh?"

"Pretty much. At least, as far as my foster mother was concerned." Lainie tilted her hand and flicked her fingers at a crumb she'd neglected to wipe off the table. "Her name was Glenda, which always reminded me of the good witch, only spelled differently. But she wasn't very good—or nice. She once called my fifth grade teacher to complain about the amount of homework I was assigned. She told Mrs. Fleming that I wouldn't be allowed to do any of it, especially the reading, until after my household chores were done. But by then, I was exhausted."

Drew reached across the table and covered her hand with his, warming it. He brushed his thumb across the top of her wrist. She suspected he meant to have a comforting effect, a calming one. But his touch spiked her pulse, arousing her senses instead.

"I'm sorry, Lainie. That must have been very difficult for you."

"It was." Her voice came out a notch above a whisper, and when she met his gaze, she spotted sympathy in his eyes. .

She was glad for the connection they'd made, for his understanding, but she didn't want his pity. She had the urge to jerk her hand away from his and to reach for the collar of her blouse. But she couldn't seem to move.

As her heart pounded a strong, steady cadence, an unfamiliar emotion rose up inside, one that stirred her senses and reminded her just how inexperienced she was. Especially when it came to things like open-hearted discussions, honest emotion and a friendship drifting toward romance.

She was at a complete loss. Should she pull her hand away from him now?

Or should she leave it in his grip forever?

Drew made the decision for her when he turned her hand over, palm side up, and clasped her fingers in his. He squeezed gently, relaying compassion and reassurance. Yet at the same time, it triggered a blood-swirling feeling she'd rather not ponder or put a name to.

"I don't think you need to worry about the Hoffmans," he said. "I have a good feeling about them. And if we all work together, I think we can boost financial support for both the Rocking Chair Ranch and Kidville."

Lainie withdrew her hand from his, albeit reluctantly. "Are you talking about the Christmas party?"

"Yes, but why stop there? What about an Easter egg decorating party, pumpkin carving... I could go on and on."

"Wow. That's creative," she said.

"Just doing my job," he said, shrugging off her compliment. Then he brightened. "You know, something tells me this is going to be a successful venture. We should celebrate."

"That's a little premature, don't you think? We haven't even toured the children's home or met the people in charge."

"Okay, then we can toast our new venture." His playful, boyish expression made it difficult to tell him no.

So Lainie returned his smile. "With a glass of milk and cookies?"

"Do you have anything better suited for adults?"

"Coffee?"

He lifted an eyebrow. "How about something stronger than caffeine?"

The wine stash. Lainie hesitated.

Oh, why not. Joy had told her to help herself.

"As a matter of fact," she said, "I do. You have your choice of merlot or chardonnay."

"Either works for me. You pick. I'll find a cork-screw."

Lainie watched Drew head for the kitchen drawer and realized this wasn't going to be a celebration. It was more of a christening, like breaking a bottle of bubbly on the bow of a ship ready to set sail for the very first time.

As she went to the cabinet and selected the merlot, she hoped that if she and Drew were about to launch a romance, it wouldn't end up a disaster of *Titanic* proportions.

Chapter Six

Lainie handed Drew the bottle of merlot, and he pulled the cork, releasing the scent of oak and blackberries.

She'd been right. It was too early to actually celebrate anything, but he'd had another motive to consider tonight a special occasion. He wanted to get to know her better, to spend some time with her, and he hadn't been able to come up with a better reason to stick around in the kitchen this evening.

She removed two wineglasses from the small hutch and set them on the table, allowing him to fill them halfway.

Then he lifted his glass in a toast. "Here's to helping the young and old alike."

"To cowboys and children." She clinked her glass against his, then took a sip.

He did the same, yet it wasn't their team effort to encourage charitable contributions for both ranches that he was thinking about. He actually liked the idea of working closely with Lainie. He liked it a lot.

"Are you looking forward to visiting Kidville?" he asked her. "Or…" He paused, realizing that her time spent in foster care might make a visit to a children's home, even one as unique as that one appeared to be, stir up bad memories. And he didn't want to open a Pandora's Box of emotion.

"I'd like to take that tour," she said softly. "Thanks for including me. Besides, it'll be good for the blog, right?"

"Yes, that's true. At this rate, we'll have enough blog content for months." He studied her face, those big brown eyes, the soft, plump lips. Her high cheekbones, like those of a top model, bore a slight blush.

Once again, it struck him that he'd seen her somewhere before. In his dreams, most likely. But in those nocturnal musings, she hadn't been dressed in baggy denim or blouses buttoned to the throat. She'd worn sexy silk panties, which she kept hidden from sight and only revealed to her lover.

"Have you started the blog yet?" she asked.

Not really. When it came to sitting down in front of his laptop and actually opening up a Word document, he'd been dragging his feet.

"I'm still conducting the interviews," he said. "I plan to talk to the younger men, too. Nate has an interesting story."

"Does he?" Lainie ran the tip of her tongue across her top lip, licking a drop of wine.

Drew sucked in a breath. For a moment, he lost his train of thought. So he focused on his wineglass. Anything but that mouth, those lips and that tongue.

"I'd heard that Nate got married recently," she said, "but not to the mother of his baby."

Oh, yeah. They'd been talking about Nate.

"You heard right," Drew said. "A few months back, a woman he'd once dated showed up here at the ranch, pregnant and battered by her new husband. She was looking for Nate and claimed the baby was his."

"How tragic." She did that thing with her tongue on her lip again, and he nearly forgot what they were talking about.

Nate and the baby. Right.

"Because of that beating, she went into premature labor," Drew said, "she gave birth to little Jessie, then died from a brain bleed."

Lainie cupped her hands around the stem of her goblet and scrunched her brow. "That poor woman. How sad."

"It sure was. Her husband is now in prison for murder." Drew reached for the bottle and replenished his wine. "More?"

She shook her head and placed her hand over the top of her glass. "What happened next?"

"Nate took custody of the baby and hooked up with Anna, the hospital social worker who'd been assigned to his case." Drew took a sip of wine. He wondered if Lainie liked the merlot. She wasn't drinking much.

She fingered the stem of the glass, her brow slightly furrowed. "Nate fell in love with his social worker?"

"Do you find that odd?"

Lainie smiled. "I can't imagine a handsome young cowboy falling for any of the ones I had as a child."

"Then Nate was lucky. Anna's both pretty and loving. But for a while, he was afraid she'd find him lacking as a father, and that he'd lose custody of the baby as a result. But he was wrong, and now they're married."

"You were right. That's an interesting story. But I have a question. You said the baby's mother 'claimed' Nate was the father. Was he?"

"At first, Nate wasn't sure. He told me that DNA didn't make a man a daddy. And that you don't have to be born into a family to belong to one."

"That's true," Lainie said, brightening. "It's an interesting take—and a good piece of advice. I'll have to keep it in mind."

"Advice? I'm not following you."

She blinked a couple times, then let out a little giggle and shrugged her shoulders. "I'm sorry. I was just thinking out loud."

And probably ruing the fact that she didn't have a family of her own. Drew was about to comment, then realized he'd be wading into a slew of emotion he didn't want to deal with. He had enough of that with Kara Lee, which had been made worse by maternal hormones. So he let it go.

He looked at Lainie's left hand, the one he'd once touched, once held. She wasn't wearing a ring, so he concluded she wasn't involved with someone.

For a man who never mixed business with pleasure, he was tempted to make an exception this time.

"Is there a special man in your life?" he asked.

"No, not anymore. Actually, there really never was. Not one who was special."

Drew sat up straighter, pumped by what sounded like good news. "That's a little surprising."

"What is?" She lifted her glass, studied the burgundy color in the kitchen light, then took a drink. "That I'm not engaged or seeing someone right now? Actually, the few men I thought were decent ended up disappointing me. I can ferret out the heart of a story, but apparently, I'm not very good at judging a man's heart and character."

"Sounds like you're recovering from a painful breakup."

Her shoulder twitched. Not quite a shrug, but a tell just the same. One that told him she'd been hurt in the past and possibly betrayed.

"I was too trusting," she said. "But I'll be a lot more careful in the future."

Drew couldn't say he blamed her. He'd built a few walls of his own, although that didn't mean he hadn't found the time for a casual but intimate relationship every now and then. And when he did, he was pretty selective.

The truth was, he found Lainie to be both attractive and completely acceptable in that regard. Would she feel the same way about him? To be blunt, would she be interested in having a short-term affair while they were both on the Rocking C?

Oh, hell. That was a crazy thought.

Lainie was the type of woman who was probably looking for a husband and kids—just like Kara Lee, who'd been on the prowl for Mr. Right and thought she'd found him in Craig Baxter.

And look how that had turned out. No, Drew didn't have any misperceptions about love and living happily ever after.

So who was he to mess with Lainie's heart?

He threw down the last of his merlot and said, "I'd better turn in for the night. Thanks for talking to me. I'll see you tomorrow."

"I'll be ready."

He returned the cork to the nearly empty bottle and placed it in the fridge. But before turning to go, a thought overtook him. "Do you have anything other than jeans or overalls to wear?"

Her brow furrowed. "Yes, why?"

"I realize we're just going to a ranch, but I told the Hoffmans you were my associate. So I thought you might want to… You know, dress the part?"

She looked down at her jeans and baggy blouse, then rolled her eyes. "Don't worry. I know how to dress professionally."

"I'm sorry. I didn't mean to offend you. In fact, you have understated class and look great no matter what you wear. Forget I said anything."

"You're forgiven." Her smile was pretty convincing. "Would business casual be acceptable?"

"That'd be perfect." He lobbed her an appreciative grin, then headed outside.

By the time he'd shut the back door, his lips had quirked into a full-on smile. Now he had something to look forward to.

And so did his nocturnal musings.

At nine o'clock on Friday morning, Brad's mother, Molly Jamison, arrived at the Rocking C Ranch driving a white Ford Taurus that had seen better days—or make that years. Lainie had been looking forward to meeting her, so she went outside to greet her in the yard.

But when a petite redhead in her midthirties climbed out of the car and pulled out a suitcase that was nearly as big as she was, Lainie's steps slowed.

Brad had to be close to twenty, so Lainie had imagined his mother to be in her forties or fifties. But she must have been a teenager when she'd given birth.

Not that it mattered. Tamping down her surprise, Lainie crossed the yard, introduced herself and reached out her hand in greeting. "It's nice to meet you. Do you need help with your luggage?"

"I don't have much," Molly said. "Just a single suitcase and an overnight bag."

Before Lainie could offer to show her where she'd be staying, Brad came out of the barn wearing a great big grin on his face. "Hey, Mom. I'm glad you're here. I'll take your stuff and put it in the cabin. I know you're eager to get a tour of the house and meet the men who live here."

"Thanks, honey." Molly blessed her son, who stood

a good six inches taller than her, with a warm smile. "I'm also ready to roll up my sleeves and help out."

"Let's start with a tour of the kitchen," Lainie said.

Molly resembled a young, red-haired Dolly Parton, but without the big hair, double Ds and the sparkle. Still, she had a sweet smile and a happy voice. Lainie liked her instantly.

She and Molly also had a lot in common, including the fact that they'd had to pull themselves up by their proverbial bootstraps, a fondness for the elderly and underprivileged children and a willingness to work.

So when it was time to go with Drew to Kidville, Lainie didn't have any qualms about leaving. The men would be in good hands with Molly.

Now, as Drew slid behind the wheel of his black pickup, which boasted all the bells and whistles, Lainie sat in the passenger seat, checking out the GPS and what appeared to be an upgraded sound system. The impressive, late-model truck had that new-car smell. At least, it did until Drew shut the driver's door, filling the cab with his faint, woodsy scent. "Ready?" He glanced across the console at Lainie, stirring her senses to the point of distraction. "Buckle up."

"You bet." But it wasn't just her body that needed to be secured with a seat belt. When it came to Drew, she feared her heart might be in for a bumpy ride.

She tried to keep her mind on the road ahead—and not on the bigger-than-life cowboy driving. But that was hard to do when he cut another glance her way, his eyes sparking. "You look great, Lainie."

Her cheeks warmed at the compliment.

"It wasn't easy to lay aside my overalls."

"Seriously?" He shot another look across the console, his brow furrowed.

She laughed, made a fist and gently punched his arm. "I'm kidding."

"Seriously," he said, "that's exactly the professional style I had in mind."

"I told you that I knew how to dress." She'd chosen a pair of low heels, black slacks and a tailored white blouse. She'd topped off her outfit with a red plaid scarf, then pulled her hair up into a topknot.

"I'm sorry for doubting you. You look great." He grinned, then winked before returning his gaze to the road ahead. A couple of miles later, he pointed to the right. "There it is. It sure looks a lot different than it did when the Clancys owned it. The perimeter used to be surrounded by rusted-out barbed wire and leaning posts. But not now. The Hoffmans have made a lot of changes to the place. If I hadn't seen pictures on the internet, I wouldn't have recognized it from before."

Lainie noted the solid, six-foot fence made of cinderblock posts and wooden slats. "It looks like they meant to protect the property and keep the children safe."

Drew turned into the driveway, where they stopped in front of a black, wrought iron gate. Using an intercom/phone system, he called the office. Once he identified himself, the doors swung open, granting them access to the property.

He continued on to a graveled lot and parked between a white minivan and a red sedan. They got out of his truck and headed for an arched entryway made of adobe brick. A wooden sign overhead read: Welcome to Kidville, Texas. Population 134.

"Do you think they have that many children living here?" Lainie asked.

"Brad said there was about a dozen, and Jim gave me the impression they'd just begun taking in kids. I think that's just their way of making Kidville sound like a real town."

She nodded, then continued along the dirt road, passing under the sign. Her steps slowed as she took in the grassy areas, a red schoolhouse, a newspaper office and even a hotel. The only areas without the quaint, Old West look were a volleyball court, a baseball field and a playground that provided a swing set, several different slides and a colorful climbing structure.

"Kidville's layout is amazing," she said. "No, it's actually mind-boggling."

"Yeah, it's pretty cool." Drew gestured for her to take the wooden sidewalk that led to the hotel.

"I've never seen anything like it." Sure, she'd watched television shows with similar settings, carefully constructed building facades and wooden sidewalks that portrayed Western life in the late 1800s. She'd also experienced living in a children's home for a while, but she'd never imagined seeing the two combined into one.

Drew had to be equally impressed because he took out his cell and began to take a picture.

"No, don't." She reached for his arm to stop him. "I would have brought my camera with me, but I'm sure they have privacy rules in place to protect the children. We should get permission from the Hoffmans first."

"Good point." Drew returned his cell to his pocket. "I hadn't thought about that. I'm glad you did."

"Where are we supposed to go?" she asked.

"Jim told me that the main office is located in the hotel, although he and his wife live in that white, two-story house next to the ball field."

Lainie spotted it right away. "Do you think all the children sleep in the house?"

"It looks big enough for some of them, but I didn't ask him about the number of kids they had or the living arrangements. Brad mentioned that his mom would be staying here, so there could be other staff members supervising children at night in some of the outbuildings."

In spite of the quaint setting, apprehension crawled through Lainie's stomach. Her thoughts drifted back to the day her caseworker had taken her from the hospital to the receiving home, where she was to complete her recovery.

She'd been walking slowly that day, more from fear and loneliness than pain. The woman had sensed her distress and had taken her hand to provide comfort and reassurance.

That lasted only about five minutes. Then Lainie was handed over to an employee who cared more about her need for a cigarette break than Lainie's need to feel safe and secure.

How odd, she thought, that those feelings would

creep back again today, as if she were being taken to a new home and to yet another, unfamiliar placement.

She wiped her palms on her slacks. When Drew's arm bumped her shoulder, she was tempted to take his hand in hers for reassurance. And it annoyed her that, at times, the past still seemed to have power over her.

"It sure is quiet," Drew said. "I wonder where all the kids are."

"Probably in school. A lot of children who come from broken, neglectful homes have never lived in an environment that encouraged education. So many of them lag behind in the classroom and struggle with their studies."

"Did you?" he asked.

"Yes, before my dad died. After that, I tended to bury my nose in a book and focus on my homework."

"Instead of boys?"

"Absolutely. Boys were a dead end." And in her experience, so were the grown-up versions for the most part. "My studies helped me forget what was going on around me." She scanned the quiet grounds. "I wonder if the kids are tutored here or if they go to a public school in town."

"Let's find out."

As she and Drew approached the hotel, a balding, heavyset man in his late fifties opened the door and came outside to welcome them. "I'm Jim Hoffman."

Drew introduced himself and Lainie, and they all shook hands.

"Come inside. My wife wants to go on the tour with

us, but she's got some business to take care of first."
Jim led the way into the hotel.

Lainie didn't know what she'd been expecting.
Something to match the exterior façade, she supposed,
but the reception area looked more like a modern living
room, with overstuffed sofas and chairs upholstered in
faux leather, a southwestern style area rug and potted
plants throughout.

A tall, slender redhead in her late fifties sat on one
of the sofas, next to a boy with messy, dark hair who
appeared to be seven or eight. She was telling him to
be patient, that he'd see his little brothers soon.

"But you don't understand." The boy's brown eyes
filled with tears. "They don't have nobody but me
to take care of them. What if someone doesn't turn
the light on for them at night? Abel is scared of the
dark. And what if they don't know how to rub Mario's
tummy when it hurts?"

"I promise to call their foster parents," the redhead
told the worried child. "I'll make sure they know what
to do."

The boy swiped at his tear-streaked face. His frown
eased a bit, but he didn't appear to be completely convinced that all would be well.

"Donna?" Jim said, "I'd like to introduce you to
Drew and Lainie, the people I told you about from the
Rocking Chair Ranch."

"It's nice to meet you." She offered them a warm
smile, then turned to the boy and placed her hand on
his small, thin shoulder. "This is Andre. Mrs. Tran,
his social worker, just brought him this afternoon to

stay with us. He's going to join us for the first part of our tour, which will be the schoolhouse, and then we'll introduce him to his new friends and teacher."

The child sniffed, then bit down on his bottom lip.

"Hey, Andre," Drew said. "It's nice to meet you."

The boy studied Drew, scanning him from his hat to his boots. Sizing him up, it seemed. "Are you a cowboy?"

Drew smiled. "Yes, I guess you could say that."

The boy's eyes widened, and his lips parted. "A *real* one?"

"Well, I grew up on a ranch. And I work with the rodeo now."

"Do you have your own horse?" the boy asked.

"I used to."

Andre's shoulders slumped, clearly disappointed. He glanced down at his sneakers, one of which was untied, then looked at Drew. "But you do know about horses, right?"

"I sure do."

The boy looked at the Hoffmans and frowned. "Mrs. Tran told me there were horses here. But that's not true. They don't have any."

"We don't have any *yet*," Donna said. "We're working on it, though."

"We do have plans to buy a couple of good riding horses in the future," Jim interjected. "But in the meantime, we have plenty of other animals, like rabbits and sheep and goats. We even have barn kittens and a couple old dogs who'll lick your face and play ball with you."

"I know," the boy said. "But..." He scrunched his face and blew out a sigh, clearly perplexed about something. Then he looked at Drew. "Can I ask you a question?"

"Sure. Go ahead."

"When people have a bad leg and can't walk too good, can they still ride a horse?"

"I'm sure they can." Drew looked at Donna, who placed her hand on Andre's small shoulder.

"When Andre was four," she explained, "he broke his foot. The bone wasn't set properly, and there wasn't any follow-up treatment. So it left him with a pronounced limp. But fortunately, we have an appointment for him to see an orthopedic surgeon next week, and we're hopeful that they'll be able to correct that for him."

"But in case they don't," Andre said, his big brown eyes seeking out Drew, "do you think I can still learn to ride someday? I want to be a cowboy when I grow up, and you can't be a very good one if you don't have a horse."

"I'll tell you what," Drew said, "if it's okay with the Hoffmans, I'd be happy to give you a riding lesson, even if I have to borrow the horse."

The boy turned to Jim. "Is it okay? Will you let me?"

"I don't see why not. I'll talk to Mr. Madison and see what we can work out. But for now, you'd better go to the schoolhouse and meet your new teacher and the other children."

Donna stood and reached for Andre's hand, helping him up. Then she walked with him to the door.

Lainie followed behind, observing the boy's uneven gait. One of his legs was clearly shorter than the other. Her heart ached for him, and she lifted her hand to finger her chest. She knew how it felt to have her medical care neglected, to face a painful surgery without anyone to offer comfort and reassurance.

Would one of the Hoffmans stay at Andre's bedside, like the loving parents of other hospitalized kids had done? She certainly hoped they would.

When they reached the red schoolhouse, they went inside. The classroom smelled of crayons and white paste, reminding Lainie of days gone by. The teacher was collecting a math worksheet from her six students—seven, now that Andre had arrived.

"This is a combination class," Jim explained while his wife led Andre to the teacher. "They're in first, second or third grade."

The teacher, a blonde in her midthirties, offered the boy a kind smile. "I'm Mrs. Wright, Andre. I heard you were coming, and I'm so glad you're here. You're just in time for recess and an afternoon snack."

After leaving Andre with his new classmates, Donna led the tour outside, letting the door close behind them.

"That poor child has had a real time of it," Donna said. "He's the oldest of three boys, and up until child protective services stepped in to rescue them from an abusive home, he did his best to look out for his younger brothers."

"Where are the other boys?" Lainie asked Donna.

"In a separate foster home. We'd like to bring them

here, but we don't have the staff or the resources to take in preschoolers yet."

"That's something else we're working on," Jim said.

Lainie hoped adding younger kids would be a priority over the horses. And that the Hoffmans would be able to take in Andre's brothers soon. It was so unfair, and the injustice of the situation sparked her into action.

"Siblings shouldn't be separated," Lainie said. "I can tell you right now, we'll do whatever we can to help you get more funding—and to provide Andre's brothers a home at Kidville."

Donna pressed her hand to her throat. "I'm overwhelmed—and so glad to hear that."

Lainie glanced at Drew, aware that he might not approve of her making a commitment like that without talking it over with him first. It would be nice to have his blessing, but she'd meant what she said. Kidville was going to be her newest project—and she hadn't even gotten the full tour.

Chapter Seven

Drew had been impressed with Jim Hoffman, even before seeing him in person, so he was ready to climb onboard. But he wouldn't have blurted out a half-baked commitment without first discussing it with his "associate."

He might have been annoyed with Lainie for making a unilateral decision for them both, but when she looked at him with those soulful brown eyes, he'd been toast.

Hell, how did a man say no to a woman like her?

Besides, Kidville was a good cause.

"Here's what I have in mind," he said, as he fell into step beside Lainie. "Rocking chairs are associated with young kids, as well as the elderly. So Esteban Enterprises can easily cross-promote Kidville and the ranch at the same time."

"Don't get me wrong," Jim said. "We'd appreciate your efforts to bring in more financial support, but I worry about splitting the pot. I'd hate to see the Rocking C only get half of what they expected."

"Actually," Drew said, "I think we'll double the pot."

Jim glanced first at his wife, who gave him a cautious nod of agreement, then back to Drew. "Then we're game if you are."

An animated smile erupted on Lainie's face. "We'd like to start by inviting your children to attend a Christmas party at the Rocking C. We'll provide the refreshments, of course. And I'll even coax one of the retired cowboys to play Santa."

That'd be a nice touch, Drew thought. He could even publish a blog post about it afterward.

Lainie continued to lay out her plan. "If it's all right to take pictures of the children, it might make the promotion more personal and touching, which would encourage potential benefactors to be more generous. Christmas and kids should be a heartwarming draw."

"You're probably right." Jim scrubbed his hand over his receding hairline. "But we have a couple of children who should stay out of the limelight, if you know what I mean. So I'd like to look over any pictures you take before they're published or posted."

"Absolutely," Lainie said. "And just so you know, I plan to propose an article for *The Brighton Valley Gazette*. That is, if you don't mind. I'd let you look it and the pictures over before we go to press."

"Well now," Jim said, "this meeting is proving to be very productive."

"I think so, too," Lainie said. "Should we schedule the party on Christmas Eve? That would give us time to decorate the ranch, buy some gifts for the children and locate a Santa Claus suit."

"That would be awesome," Donna said. "Some of our children have never had a real Christmas."

"I know." Lainie's voice was soft and almost fragile. "I spent a few years in foster homes when I was a girl. And some of the kids I grew up with had sad backgrounds."

"I'm sorry to hear that," Donna said.

Lainie shrugged. "It's all in the past. But that's why I want to help your kids now."

Drew was a little surprised she'd been so forthcoming, but then again, the Hoffmans were an easy couple to like and to trust.

"I hope we can get some donations rolling in quickly," Lainie added. "I'd like to see you be able to bring Andre's brothers here as soon as possible."

Donna placed her hand on Lainie's arm. "Believe me, Jim and I want to see that happen, too, but since you're no stranger to foster care, you probably have an idea how long these things can take. It's not just the funding we need, it's licensing and paperwork, too. I'm afraid you'll have to be patient until Jim and I work through the system."

Lainie's cheeks turned a deep shade of pink. "Yes, of course. Sometimes I let my heart and enthusiasm run away with me."

Drew realized she was eager to see Andre's family reunited because, after losing touch with her twin sister, she knew how the poor kid felt. He could certainly understand that. He felt sorry for Andre, too, but for a different reason. He admired the wannabe cowboy's loyalty to his younger brothers and his determination to look out for them.

Family came first. Drew understood that. His mom might have passed away, but he was committed to looking out for his sister—whether she was a preschooler or a grown woman—for the rest of their lives.

"Let's continue the tour." Jim led them toward the barn. "Like I said, we don't have any horses yet, but I'll show you what we do have. We've done a lot of research on animal therapy and have put it to work here. It's a big part of our program."

Donna chimed in. "Each child will have their own animal to look after, which will give them something to love. And it will also teach them responsibility."

Twenty minutes later, after seeing two frisky Australian shepherds, four fluffy kittens, a chicken coop called the Peep-Peep Palace, a mama duck and her ducklings, as well as goats and sheep, the tour ended.

Lainie and Drew thanked the Hoffmans and promised to be in touch soon. Then they climbed into the pickup and headed back to the Rocking C.

They'd barely gone a mile down the road when Drew glanced across the seat and spotted Lainie sporting a grin.

"You sure look happy," he said.

"You're right. Helping the Hoffmans and those children has given me a real purpose."

"You've got good instincts. I'll give you that much."

Her smile deepened. "Thank you."

"However, don't ever pull a stunt like that again."

Her brow furrowed, and she cocked a sideways glance at him. "What are you talking about?"

"In the professional world, we don't offer services until we've discussed them with the entire team. Lucky for you, I agreed wholeheartedly with your idea and plan to run it past my boss for his approval. But if I'd had any qualms, I would have had to do some fancy backpedaling, and then we'd both look like idiots."

Her once happy expression sobered. "I'm sorry. You're right."

"Don't get me wrong," he said, "I appreciate your enthusiasm, and I'm glad supporting the Hoffmans and Kidville gives you a sense of purpose, but it's not the same for me. Promoting them is my *job*."

"I'm sorry if I overstepped. I shouldn't have used the word *we*."

A pang of guilt, as well as sympathy, lanced his chest. He hadn't meant to scold her, especially since this was more than a job to her. But he couldn't get carried away with soft, tender feelings—especially for Lainie. He had enough to worry about without taking another waif under his wing.

Yet just looking at her now, seated next to him in the truck, her eyes bright and focused on whatever she had on her mind, he wouldn't consider her vulnerable. She looked strong, proud...and lovable.

Whoa. Don't even go there. Drew returned his focus to the road. He'd better watch his step when he was around Lainie. Not to mention his heart.

* * *

In spite of being reprimanded by her "business associate" for being unprofessional, Lainie entered the house with her heart nearly bursting and her head abuzz with holiday plans. She'd thought she might be too excited to eat. That is, until she took her first step into the mudroom and the warm aroma of tomatoes, garlic and basil accosted her.

Molly stood at the stove, holding a wooden spoon in one hand and a potholder in the other.

"Something sure smells good," Lainie said. "Thanks for covering for me."

"You're welcome. I love to cook." Molly lowered the flame, then turned away from the pot simmering on the stove. "How'd the tour go?"

"Oh, my gosh." Lainie wasn't sure she could put her thoughts and feelings into words. "Kidville is amazing."

Molly burst into a smile. "That's exactly how I felt after my first visit. I'm so glad I get to work there."

"I can see why." Lainie scanned the kitchen. "Need any help?"

"No, I've got it all under control. But do you mind keeping an eye on the spaghetti sauce for a couple of minutes? I forgot to give Brad a letter that came in yesterday's mail, and he's waiting for it."

"No problem. Take your time."

Molly had no more than shut the back door, when the telephone rang. Lainie answered and was surprised to hear Mr. Carlton's voice on the other end.

"I've gotta tell you," the editor said. "If you continue to turn in quality columns like the one we just published, I might have to hire an answering service to handle all the calls we're receiving from Dear Debbie fans. I told you they're pretty vocal, and this time they weren't complaining. They like the direction the column is going. Of course, we did change the font and the layout."

Seriously? He was taking credit for the positive reader response?

Okay, so the advice she'd given had come from the mouth of a wise old man. But Lainie had written the column herself, using her own words, and she was going to stake a claim on some of that success, if not all of it.

"We also made it easier to find the column—right next to the obituaries." He chuckled. "Kind of apropos, don't you think? Life's a bitch, and then you die."

Lainie went silent. Did she really want to work for this guy?

"Just a little editorial humor, kid. But I'm glad Dear Debbie is finally back on track."

"Thanks. It's nice to know that you and the readers like what I've done. I also want to give you a heads-up about something else. I'm sending you a proposal for an article about a local children's home called Kidville. I took a tour, and it was impressive."

"I've heard about that place. What do you have in mind?"

She told him more—about the unique setting, the administrators and their animal therapy plan. But just enough to whet his appetite.

"Send me that proposal," he said, giving her the green light she'd been hoping for.

When the call ended, she was tempted to hole up in her room and outline her proposal, but she couldn't neglect the Dear Debbie column when she was on a roll. And that meant she'd have to come up with a clever answer to at least one of the latest letters.

Lainie had just checked the spaghetti sauce when Molly returned to the kitchen.

"What else can I do to help?" Lainie asked.

"Actually, not much. The tables are set, and I have everything else under control."

It certainly looked like it. The salad was made and in a bowl on the counter. The garlic bread was wrapped in foil and ready to pop into the oven.

"Are you sure?" Lainie asked.

"Absolutely."

"Then if you don't mind, I'll take off for a while, but I'll be back to help you serve dinner."

"Take your time."

Lainie thanked her, then with her confidence bolstered by Mr. Carlton's phone call, she slipped off to her room to look over the latest Dear Debbie letters.

Only trouble was, five minutes turned to ten, and as the tick-tocks of the windup clock on the bureau grew louder and louder, she feared she was going to be a one-column wonder.

There was, however, one letter that struck an interesting chord. It had been written by a woman who'd dreamed of getting married, creating a home of her own and having babies.

I met a great guy at work and was immediately attracted to him. He's sweet, funny and cute. I couldn't believe someone hadn't snatched him up already, and before long, I fell head over heels for him.

And that's my problem. I just found out that he's a widower with four small children.

If I marry him, I'd have to give up my dream of having a family of my own.

Lainie understood the woman's dream as well as her dilemma, but she sympathized with those poor, motherless kids. Her first impulse was to tell the woman that the two adults involved would have to be fully committed to the children or everyone would be miserable.

I fell head over heels for him…

Did she love the man enough to be his life partner? To join his team and mother those children as her own? It was impossible to know.

Lainie blew out a sigh. Doling out the wrong advice would be devastating.

What would Sully tell the woman? She glanced at the clock on the bureau. There was no time to ask him now. It was almost five o'clock, so she shut down her laptop and left it in her room. Then she went to help Molly serve the meals.

When she entered the kitchen, the young ranch hands had already gathered, and Brad was introducing them to his mom.

But it wasn't Molly or the cowboys who caught Lainie's eye. It was Drew, who stood off to the side, leaning against the doorjamb, his arms crossed in an alluring, masculine pose. When his gaze zeroed in on her, any plans she might have had scattered to the wayside.

"Got a minute?" he asked.

For him? She was tempted to say, "I've got all night." Instead, she nodded and let him lead her out to the front porch.

Once Drew and Lainie stepped outside and out of earshot, she asked, "What's up?"

"I'm not sure if you had a chance to speak to any of the nurses yet, but Chloe Martinez called a few minutes ago. She and her husband Joe own the Rocking C and plan to be home for Christmas. So I mentioned our plan to host a party for the kids."

"What'd she say?"

"Chloe loved the idea. In fact, she'd like to help pull it all together, but she and Joe are just finishing up their graduate programs at the university in Houston, and they can't leave school until the twenty-third."

"So the party's still on." Lainie beamed, her enthusiasm impossible to ignore. "That's awesome. There isn't any reason we can't get started with the planning and prep work."

"I guess not, but there could be a few bumps in the road."

Lainie's smile paled, and her lips parted. "What do you mean?"

"There's no telling what the old guys will think about it. Some of them, like Rex and Gilbert, can get a little crotchety. They might not appreciate having a bunch of children running around."

"Seriously? You think they'd be upset?"

Drew hadn't meant to steal her happiness, but he'd wanted to warn her of the possibility so she wouldn't be disillusioned if things didn't work out the way she wanted them to. He'd had his share of disappointing holidays.

"There's no way to know how they'll react until we tell them," he said. "And the sooner the better."

Lainie nodded, worry etched on her face.

He placed a hand on her shoulder to offer support and comfort. "Come on, let's go."

Then as he guided her into the house, his hand slipped around her in a show of solidarity. At least, that's what he told himself he was doing as they continued to the dining room, where the retired cowboys sat around the table.

"While you're all together," Drew said, "we wanted to share something we have in the works." He glanced at Lainie, who was biting down on her lower lip, which he found arousing. And distracting, so his words stalled for a beat.

Fortunately, Lainie shook off whatever apprehension she'd been having and spoke up for both of them. "Earlier this afternoon, Drew and I visited a home for abused and neglected children that's located a few miles down the road."

"You mean the one at the old Clancy place?" Sully asked.

"Yes, that's it." Lainie went on to sing the praises of

the Hoffmans and their innovative home. "So we had this brilliant idea about hosting a Christmas party for those kids here on the Rocking C."

Drew's hand slipped from her shoulder, his fingers trailing along her back until he drew away and moved closer to the table. "What do you say, guys?"

"Christmas is a lot more fun when little tykes are around," Gilbert said. "We'd better get a bigger tree than that scrawny stick we had last year."

Rex agreed. "My Jennilyn used to make a big deal out of decorating the house, baking all kinds of sweets and wrapping gifts. And that reminds me, we ought to have something under that tree for those kids."

"How many are living there?" Gilbert asked. "It might be nice if we took up a collection, then sent someone shopping for us."

At that, Sully chimed in. "I'm pretty good at wrapping. A few years back, I helped the local Four H Club at their gift wrapping booth they had at the Wexler mall."

"I'm glad to hear you're onboard," Lainie told Sully.

"Hey," he said. "I like kids."

"Good," Lainie said, "because you'd make a perfect Santa."

"Ain't that the truth?" Rex howled with laughter. "And Sully won't need any stuffing around his middle, either."

Sully puffed out his chest. "I'd be delighted to be Santa Claus." Then he turned to Rex. "I'd rather have a little meat and muscle on me than look like a bony ol' scarecrow."

Gilbert slapped his hand on the table and let out a hoot. "Now there's an idea. If we host a Halloween party for those kids, we can prop Rex up in the cornfield and let him play the part."

Lainie's excitement lit her pretty face. "You guys are the best, you know that?"

"Ah, shucks," Sully said. "No, we aren't."

"Speak for yourself, Sully," Gilbert said. "I'm thinking I'm pretty dang good."

Drew couldn't help but laugh at the men's humor. When Lainie looked at him, he gave her a wink.

And not just because their Christmas party was a go. If he had his way, promoting Kidville and the Rocking Chair Ranch wasn't the only joint venture they'd start up.

Four days later, Drew shook his head in disbelief. Somehow, he'd let Lainie rope him into making Christmas cookies.

"You do realize it's still more than a week before the party." He draped the red-and-white checkered apron she'd suggested he wear over the back of a chair. He didn't mind assuming kitchen duties. Heck, he'd done most of the cooking and cleaning after his mom got sick. But he'd never dressed the part. "I don't know why we have to bake cookies tonight."

"Because there's so much to do at the last minute." She sprinkled flour on the open breadboard, then handed him a rolling pin. "And this is something we can do ahead of time."

"But the cookies won't taste very good if they aren't fresh."

She didn't seem the least bit concerned. "I plan to freeze them and thaw them the night before the party. Don't worry. I know what I'm doing." Then she reached out, touched his forearm and smiled. "You agreed to help me, remember? You said you'd do anything that needed to be done."

"Yes, but when I made that offer, I was thinking more along the lines of getting the tree and decorating it."

"You can do that, too."

He'd had every intention of doing his part and more. He just hadn't expected to work in the kitchen. Or to be swayed into doing so by the singe of Lainie's touch or the warmth of her smile.

She placed a lump of dough on the floured board. "I appreciate your help. Do you know how to do this?"

"I'll manage." He'd seen his mom make biscuits before. And once, while she'd been on chemo and sicker than a dog, he'd stepped in and taken over for her. They'd purchased the heat-and-serve variety at the grocery store after that.

Lainie unscrewed the lid of a mason jar to use for cutting out circles. "I wish I had some real cookie cutters. Then we could make trees and stars and other Christmas shapes. But this time, plain round ones will have to do." She pointed to the lumpy side of the dough. "Roll it out evenly or the cookies will be lopsided."

Okay, boss." Drew rolled out the dough flat and

even, but the edges were cracked. "Am I doing this right?"

Lainie took a moment to look over his work. "That's perfect." She handed him the jar lid. "Make the circles as close together as you can."

He followed her instructions, then placed them on the pan.

"Let's get the first batch in the oven," she said, setting the timer.

He glanced at the large mixing bowl on the counter. They'd hardly made a dent in the dough. "How many of these are we going to make?"

"Dozens and dozens. I love frosted sugar cookies, don't you?" She didn't wait for his answer and went back to work, her holiday excitement impossible to ignore.

It was also easy to appreciate. She had a girlish look to her, not to mention a little flour on her nose. Yet at the same time—maybe it was the yellow gingham apron she wore—he saw a domestic goddess.

Lainie was going to make a good wife and mother. A pretty one. He imagined coming home each night after work and finding her in the kitchen, preparing his meals, and a zing shot through him.

He quickly shook off the thought. Was he nuts? Bumping elbows with her tonight was one thing. But words like *permanent*, *long-term* and *forever* weren't in his vocabulary.

Before long, a sweet cookie aroma filled the room. After Lainie pulled the first pan from the oven and re-placed it with the next, she removed powdered sugar and a bottle of vanilla from the pantry. Then she took milk from the fridge and placed it on the counter, next to a cube of butter that was already softening.

From the amount of dough still in the mixing bowl, Drew figured they were going to have a boatload of cookies, yet Lainie measured out only a small amount of powdered sugar.

He studied her as she worked. She still had a dusting of flour on her nose, although she wasn't aware of it. And her sweet smile made him smile, too.

"Aren't you going to frost all of them?" he asked.

"Not the ones we're going to serve at the party. I'll do that the night before."

"I don't understand."

"I'm going to frost a couple of them now. Don't you want to see how the finished product is going to look and taste?"

Actually, Drew loved sweets. "Sure. Why not?" He watched as she whipped up the frosting in a bowl with a handheld mixer, then she added a couple drops of green food coloring and blended it together with a spoon.

"Mama Kate used to make the best cookies," Lainie said.

"Your first foster mom, right?"

Lainie nodded. "She always let me help her since I didn't play outside with the other kids."

Drew could understand why a girl might prefer time in the kitchen, cooking and baking. But by the way Lainie had said it, he got the idea that she rarely went outdoors. "Did you prefer being indoors?"

The spoon she'd been using to mix the frosting

stilled, then she started stirring again. "Back then, I wasn't really able to."

A bad memory? Or maybe it was just a simple, heartfelt reflection of the days she'd lived with Mama Kate and it made her sad.

He told himself it really didn't matter which, but for some reason, it did. "Why not?"

At first, she didn't answer and continued to mix the frosting. A couple of beats later, she said, "I was a little sickly back then."

She'd mentioned something about having health issues, but he hadn't considered them serious. "You mean, from an illness?"

She clicked her tongue and continued stirring. "It was no big deal. It's all in the past."

He was about to quiz her further, but she switched the subject on him as swiftly as a champion stock car driver shifted gears and changed lanes.

"Donna gave me a list with the children's names, ages and sizes," she said. "The men chipped in to buy gifts for them, and I volunteered to do the shopping. Do you want to go with me?"

"Not on a bet."

She laughed at his quick and telling response. But he didn't mind. He liked the sound of her laughter, the lilt of her voice.

"I hate to shop," he said.

"But you dress so well."

"That's different. I go to my favorite men's store sometimes, but not all that often. There's a clerk who works there and knows what I like. So I usually just give her a call and bam. Done. But in general, I'm not into shopping."

"Why?"

He shrugged. "When my mom was sick, that job fell on me. So I've always considered it a chore."

"But one that needs to be done." Lainie dripped more food coloring into the bowl. "You were responsible—and a good son. I'll bet your mom was proud of you."

"She was, but she hated having to rely on me to do everything." Drew could still remember her stretched out on the living room sofa, weak and pale and only a wisp of the woman she'd once been. Tears streaming down her cheek as she apologized for not being strong enough to take care of him and his sister anymore.

"I'm sure she enjoyed being your mom and felt badly when she had to give it up. That's how I'd feel, if I were a mother."

Drew glanced at Lainie, who had a maternal air about her this evening, especially when she wore an apron and baked cookies.

"Do you plan to have kids?" he asked.

"Yes, someday. But for now, I have the children at Kidville."

He was glad she'd taken those kids under her wing. She was clearly eager to make them happy. He suspected she'd do the same with her own someday.

She turned to him with a spoonful of green frosting in her hand. "Here, try a bite."

He opened his mouth and relished the creamy, sweet taste bursting on his tongue.

"What do you think?" she asked.

"It's good." He withdrew a clean spoon from the drawer, dipped it into the small mixing bowl and offered it to her. "Your turn."

"Okay." Her mouth opened and closed around the spoon, tasting it herself. Then she ran the tip of her tongue over her lips.

His knees went weak, and an almost overwhelming urge rose up inside, pressing him to take her in his arms and kiss her. But he couldn't do that. He shouldn't, anyway, so he tamped down the compulsion the best he could.

Still, he continued to study her.

"Hmm, this is really good." Her voice came out soft. Sweet. Smooth.

He couldn't help himself; he reached out and brushed the flour from the tip of her nose. Their gazes locked. Her pretty brown eyes darkened, and her lips parted.

His heart pumped hard and steady, and his hand stilled. The temptation to kiss her senseless rose up again, stronger than ever. But he wouldn't do that.

He shouldn't, anyway.

Yet as he struggled to do the right thing, the smart thing, desire trumped common sense.

Chapter Eight

Drew cupped Lainie's jaw, and his thumb caressed her cheek. Now was the time to release her and apologize for making such an intimate move, such a presumptive one, but the moment dissipated in a heartbeat.

Her lips parted a little wider. Whether it was in anticipation or surprise, he wasn't quite sure. But at this point, he didn't care which it was—as long as she didn't stop him. He set the spoon on the counter.

At least, he tried to. It clattered to the floor, but neither of them looked anywhere but at each other.

He took her in his arms, bent his head and lowered his mouth to hers.

The kiss was hot, yet sweet. And the taste? Sugar and vanilla and everything a man ever craved.

His tongue swept into her mouth. Her breath caught,

but she didn't pull away. Instead, she clung to him as if she might collapse if she didn't.

The kiss intensified, and so did his hunger. He couldn't seem to get enough of her taste, enough of *her*. He might have suggested that she go with him to the privacy of the cabin if he hadn't heard approaching footsteps and someone clearing their throat.

Lainie damn near jumped through the roof as she broke away from Drew's embrace, landing on the tip of the spoon and sending it sliding toward the doorway and ending at Sully's feet.

The jovial old man grinned from ear to ear. With his white hair and beard and wearing a red-and-green plaid shirt, he looked a lot like old St. Nick himself. Just the sight of him put a new spin on the old tune of "I saw Mommy Kissing Santa Claus."

In this case, it was Santa Sully who'd gotten the romantic eyeful.

"Hey, kids." Sully looked around the kitchen. "What's cooking?"

Besides Drew's blood pressure?

"I'm…sorry," Lainie said, lightly touching her lips. Her fingers trailed down to her collar. The top button of her blouse, barely visible under her apron, had come undone, and she fumbled to close it up tight. It was almost as if she was trying to hide behind that blouse, just as she'd hidden the pink, sexy panties under the denim overalls the day of the mouse encounter.

Drew would give just about anything to know why she seemed compelled to cover up. Was she wearing skimpy undies now?

"What are you sorry for?" Sully asked her, as he stooped to pick up the spoon. He set it on the counter, then turned to them with a big ol' grin that sparked a Santa-like glimmer in his eyes. Even his chuckle had a ho-ho-ho quality about it.

"Because I'm supposed to be working." Lainie quickly turned her back to them, reached for a cookie on the cooling rack that sat on the counter and showed it to Sully. "Would you like one? I'd be happy to frost it for you."

"Don't mind if I do," the oldster said. "I came down here looking for a bedtime snack. And a sweet one sounds pretty darn good."

Lainie got right on it, frosting not one but two cookies and handing them both to Sully. She waited while he wolfed one of them down.

"What do you think?" she asked.

"They're great. Best I've had in ages."

"Too bad I didn't have a Christmas tree cookie cutter."

Sully chomped into the second cookie. "You could call these ornaments."

"You're right."

As Lainie and Sully launched into a conversation about baking, the tree decorating and the gifts she planned to purchase and wrap for the kids, Drew retreated to the sink and started washing the bowls.

To him, it was just a bunch of nervous jabber, an attempt to put the kiss behind them and to pretend it hadn't happened. But it *had*.

And if it had the same effect on her that it had on him, it wasn't one either of them was likely to forget.

More than twelve hours had passed since the cookie baking session turned into a romantic moment and ended with an earth-shaking kiss. Yet Drew's memory of Lainie's sweet taste and the feel of her body in his arms hadn't faded a bit.

He'd tried to broach the subject with her after Sully left the kitchen last night, but she hadn't wanted to talk about it. She claimed she wasn't feeling well, that she needed to get some sleep and that she'd finish the baking in the morning.

She had looked a little tired. It was hard to say for sure, but he suspected, in reality, she was both shaken and troubled by the kiss.

He could understand why. He'd been stunned by it, too. But since he hadn't been ready to face any of those *now what* questions, especially when he didn't have an answer, he'd counted himself lucky and had gone back to his cabin.

All during breakfast, Lainie had bustled about the kitchen, but she'd hardly glanced his way. And the only thing she'd said to him was, "Good morning."

Even when Sully came in from the dining room for a second cup of coffee and thanked her for a tasty meal, she'd followed it up with a simple, "You're welcome."

Her cheeks bore a constant flush, though. So he decided the only thing bothering her was that kiss.

It might have been an ornery move on Drew's part,

but he'd set up an after-breakfast interview with Sully in the kitchen.

He doubted Lainie'd like having both men return to the scene of the passionate crime, but after Sully went on his way, Drew would broach the subject. And who knew? He might even instigate another kiss.

But things hadn't worked out the way he'd planned. Moments after Sully took a seat at the table and Drew poured them each a cup of coffee, Lainie slipped out of the kitchen and didn't return.

"Something's bothering Lainie," Sully said. "Is she upset because you kissed her last night? Or just about being caught?"

"I'm not sure." Drew took a sip of coffee. "Some women aren't easy to figure out. And Lainie's one of them. But just for the record, I don't have any regrets. It was a great kiss."

"She certainly seemed to be enjoying it," Sully said. "My guess is that she's not sure what to do about it."

Drew wasn't, either. But that didn't mean he wouldn't like to kiss her again. Lainie was proving to be... Well, intriguing, to say the least.

"I really like that little gal," Sully said.

"I do, too." Drew stared at his coffee for a second. "What do you know about her?"

Sully lifted his mug, blew at the steam rising from the top and took a sip. "Not much. She's a sweetheart. Pretty, too. But her friends are a little iffy."

"Seriously? That surprises me."

"Yeah, me, too. But it's probably because she has a big heart. Too big, I suspect."

"What do you mean?"

Sully sat back in his chair. "It's nothing, I guess. It's just that, over the last couple weeks, she's come to me with one question or another. It seems that either one of her girlfriends or someone she knows has a problem, usually due to their own making." Sully slowly shook his head. "I gotta tell you, Lainie really needs to choose some new friends. Some of them don't have the sense the Good Lord gave a goose."

Was that a red flag? Had Sully spotted a flaw in Lainie that Drew had failed to notice? Or were her questionable friendships merely the sign of a warm, loving heart? Either way, Drew intended to find out.

Sully clucked his tongue. "I guess everyone has a weakness."

"You're right." And Drew figured some of them also harbored a few secrets.

For a while the men didn't say anything.

"Cookies aside," Sully said, "how're the party plans coming along?"

"Everything seems to be on track."

"Say," Sully said, "I was thinking. Why don't we wrap up that Christmas party with a good, old-fashioned hayride and a sing-along? The church my wife and I used to attend would have one each summer to celebrate the children's promotion to their Sunday school classes. And we all had a lot of fun."

"Good idea. The kids would probably like that."

"There's an old wagon in the barn," Sully said. "You should check it out. It's probably an antique by now and hasn't been used in years. So you'd need to clean it up and fill it with straw. They don't have any draft horses on the Rocking C, but you could hitch it up to the John Deere. Might be a good idea to mention it to Nate and see if he agrees."

"Yeah. I'll share the idea with Lainie, too."

That's not all Drew would like to share with her, but for the time being, his romantic plans had hit the skids.

That might not be a bad thing. Maybe he should back off for a while—or at least, take things slow and steady.

Yet that didn't mean he wouldn't dream about her tonight and relive that sweet, arousing kiss all over again.

Lainie stood in the kitchen, chopping celery, pickles and hard-boiled eggs to mix into the potato salad she was preparing for lunch. But her mind wasn't on her work. It was on that luscious, romantic moment she'd shared with Drew in this very room last night. A tingle raced up her leg to the back of her neck.

As he'd held her in his arms and kissed her senseless, she'd completely lost her head until Sully interrupted them. At that point, she'd finally returned to earth. Yet even now, she wasn't back on solid ground, and she didn't know what to do about it.

One kiss would surely lead to a second, but then what?

Dread picked at her. She wasn't ready for an intimate relationship—and not just because of that horrible debacle at that hotel lounge in Houston, when Craig Baxter's wife caught him and Lainie together and assumed the worst.

Lainie didn't blame Kara Baxter for thinking that her husband had a lover. To be honest, that's the direction the relationship had been heading, but Lainie had been reluctant to become intimate. And for good reason.

She fingered her chest, felt along the cotton fabric that hid the raised ridge. In college, her first real boyfriend and almost-lover had balked at the sight of the long pink scar.

"Why didn't you warn me?" he'd asked.

She'd cried, and he'd apologized, but the whole evening had turned out to be disappointing and they'd broken up. After that, she'd vowed to be more careful with her affections.

Then Craig came along, and she'd decided to give him a chance. Looking back at the way things had ended between them, she thanked her lucky stars—and her ugly scar—that she hadn't let him convince her to make love.

But tell that to the world. While the cell phone cameras focused on Craig and his pregnant wife, Lainie had rushed to her car in the parking lot, but she hadn't been able to outrun the internet. By nine o'clock the next morning, the scene had gone viral, the comments devastating. You'd think people would consider Craig the villain, but they seemed more focused on how he hovered over his wife, how he cooed to her, caressed her...

And that left Lainie to take all the heat. Even the blogosphere and all the network gossip shows got on the bandwagon, leaving her both hurt and angry.

She took out her frustration on a stalk of celery, chopping it hard and nicking her finger in the process.

"Ouch!" She tossed the paring knife in the sink.

See? That's what happens when you let your emotions get in the way of good sense. You screw up.

She sucked her finger, the metallic taste of blood lingering like a bad memory and an unearned reputation as a temptress and a home wrecker, when all she'd ever wanted was to love and be loved.

Now, here she was, considering another attempt at a relationship.

Was Drew different from Craig? Could she trust him to see past her scar and into her heart? Quite frankly, she wasn't sure, but she was tempted to give him the benefit of the doubt and risk being hurt again.

She glanced down at the flannel and denim she'd pulled out of the closet after her morning shower. She'd kept her curls contained in a topknot, but on a whim, she'd applied a coat of pink lip gloss and a little mascara.

It felt good to tap into her femininity again. Maybe it was time to start dressing the part. She might not have the money to buy expensive clothes, but she'd always been style conscious. And she wasn't going to wear loose tops and baggy pants the rest of her life.

For now, though, she'd focus on preparing lunch.

"Hey, Lainie?"

She turned toward the doorway, where Drew stood, his hair stylishly mussed, and wearing a dazzling smile. Why did he have to be so appealing?

Drew made his way into the kitchen. "Sully had

a suggestion for the party. What do you think about wrapping up the festivities with a hayride and a sing-along?"

"I think that's a great idea."

"There's an old wagon behind the barn. We'd have to clean it up, but it should work out perfectly for what we have in mind. Do you want to see it?"

"Absolutely." She turned to the sink, and washed her hands then grabbed a dish towel to dry them. "Let me put the potato salad in the refrigerator."

Minutes later, they'd left the house and walked around the barn, where a large, buckboard style wagon was parked on a thick patch of grass in the back.

"This is it," Drew said.

At first glance, it looked to be about a hundred years old and weather-beaten. It didn't just need a good cleaning, it could use a coat of paint, too.

"It has potential," she said.

"I've already checked out the structure, and it looks all right. One of the wood slats on the side needs to be replaced, but with a little work, it'll do just fine."

"The kids are going to love a hayride, especially Andre. I'll bet he'll be in seventh heaven."

"I was thinking about him," Drew said. "The next time I'm in town, I'm going to buy him a child-size cowboy hat."

Lainie leaned her hip against the wagon's open tail-gate and gazed at him. "That'd be really sweet. I'm sure he'd love it."

He shrugged a single shoulder. "I figured he would."

"You know," she said, pressing her palm on the open

tailgate and finding it sturdy, "you promised to let him ride a horse. He'll be disappointed if it doesn't work out for some reason."

"I know. That's why I've already talked to Nate about it. He suggested we use a gentle mare named Felicity."

Lainie hopped up on the tailgate and took a seat. "I'd planned to call the Hoffmans later today to talk about the party plans. If it's okay with you, I'll ask them if Andre can come here before the party to ride Felicity."

"Sure, go ahead. I'd be happy to work around their schedule."

"Then if they don't have any objections, I'll set up a day and time that works for everyone."

Drew continued to study her, his gaze sweeping her face. "You're something else, Lainie."

She wasn't entirely sure what he meant, but her chest warmed and her heart fluttered at what was surely a compliment. She crossed her ankles and swayed her legs, a nervous reaction that might seem a little girl-ish, but there was something very grown up about what she was feeling—and about the way Drew was looking at her.

"There's something else I wanted to bring up while we're out here alone," he added.

Uh-oh. Here it comes. The kiss chat she'd been dreading. Yet for some reason, she wasn't the least bit worried about having it now.

"It was fun last night. I'd like to finish what we started."

Was he talking about the kiss? Or the baking session? Either way, she didn't dare ask.

"After that," he said, "maybe we can roll out the remaining dough and make more cookies."

Heat singed her cheeks, and her heartbeat kicked up to a lively pace. So he'd been referring to the kiss. She was tempted to slip off the tailgate and make a mad dash to the house, but before she could move, Drew closed in on her, blocking her escape route.

"I hadn't meant for that to happen," she said, "but it…just did."

"It was a nice kiss, don't you think?"

That's not how she'd describe it. She'd use words like *sweet, arousing* and *sensual*.

"Just *nice*?" she asked.

"Actually…" His lips quirked into a crooked grin. "On a scale of one to ten? I'd rate it an eleven or twelve."

Now it was her turn to smile. "Something tells me you've had plenty of kisses to compare it to, so I'll take your word for it."

"You haven't?" he asked.

She wasn't about to admit that she lacked any real experience worth counting. "I thought it was pretty good."

"Good enough to try it again someday?"

She ought to tell him no, to set up some boundaries between them, to protect herself from entering another bad relationship, but she couldn't deny the truth.

"Sure," she said. "Maybe someday."

He closed the two-foot gap between them, which seemed to be his way of saying, *Then why not now?*

For the life of her, she couldn't come up with a single objection.

He placed his right hand along her jaw. His fingers slipped under her ear and reached the back of her neck. The pad of his thumb caressed her cheek, scrambling her brain and setting her senses on high alert. All the while, he studied her face as if he could read every single detail about her life, every memory in her heart.

Lainie could've sworn he was going to kiss her again, and she wasn't sure what to do about it—if anything.

Fight? Flight?

Or should she just roll with it?

Preparing to make a move of some kind, she placed her palms on the tailgate and shifted her weight. As she sat back down, one side of the tailgate cracked and her seat gave way. She let out a scream, grabbed Drew and brought him crashing to the ground with her.

Chapter Nine

Drew had been blessed with quick reflexes, but when the wood cracked and the bracket broke, he didn't have much time to react.

He tried to catch Lainie, as her fingernails dug into his arm, but she still slid down the slanting tailgate, pulling him to the ground with her.

He rolled to the side, thankful for the thick patch of long grass that softened their landing, and propped himself up on his elbow. He hovered over her, brushed a silky strand of hair from her face and searched her eyes. "Are you okay?"

"I think so." She blinked a couple of times. "Nothing hurts."

"Good." He probably ought to help her up, but he liked being stretched out beside her, gazing at her pretty face, taunted by her soft floral scent. It was an arousing position.

Admittedly, there were better, more romantic places for a proverbial roll in the hay than a patch of grass, next to an old buckboard wagon, but he wasn't about to suggest a change in position, let alone location. Not while he had Lainie in his arms again. He felt compelled to kiss her long and hard.

He really shouldn't. But she was studying him intently, practically inviting him to do it.

When her lips parted, he was toast.

As their lips met and his eyes closed, they returned to that blissful, intimate state they'd reached last night. Their bodies naturally took off from where they'd left off.

Drew rolled her with him to the side, finding a comfortable spot away from the wagon, and continued to kiss her thoroughly. Tongues mated, breaths mingled and hearts pounded out in need.

He stroked her back, his hands bunching up the flannel fabric that separated his fingers from her skin. But a simple article of clothing, no matter how blousy, couldn't hide the soft, feminine body underneath.

He slid his hands along the curve of her spine and down the slope of her hips. As his mouth continued its gentle yet demanding assault, Lainie let out a soft whimper, sending a rush of desire coursing through his veins.

Unable to help himself, he slipped his hand under the hem of her shirt, seeking the woman inside. As he felt along her warm skin and explored the curve of her waist, his testosterone flared. He inched his way up to the edge of her satin bra, soft and sleek, and sought her breast. But the moment he cupped the full mound, she jerked away as if he'd crossed an invisible line.

And hadn't he? Considering the circumstances, where they were and how they came to be there, she probably thought he was way off base.

She'd seemed more than willing, though. That is, until now.

"I'm sorry," he said. "I guess I got a little carried away."

She sat up, lifted her hand to her collar, fingering the flannel fabric, and slowly shook her head. "No, I'm the one who should be sorry. I didn't mean to overreact. I hope you don't think I was being a tease."

A flush covered her throat, indicating her own arousal. She bit down on her lip, which was still plump from the gentle assault of their kiss. "It's just that…" She scanned the area around them. "This isn't the time or the place."

She had a point, but he made light of it by tossing her a playful grin, hoping to ease her discomfort or embarrassment. "Well, the timing was okay with me. And I admit this probably isn't the place. But no one saw us, so we're the only ones who know what happened."

She got to her feet and, after righting her shirt, she pointed at the wagon. "I think, once that tailgate is fixed, this will work out perfectly for what we have in mind."

He wasn't about to mention what *he'd* had in mind,

what he was still thinking, but he followed her lead and rose from the grassy ground.

"Or better yet," she said, "maybe we should ask around the neighboring ranches and see if we can borrow something similar."

Avoiding a person or a subject seemed to be her primary line of defense.

His first thought was to mention it, to take her back to the subject at hand, but it was probably in his best interests to let it go for now. Did he really want to talk about what they'd just done and what it might mean?

He was definitely attracted to her. And the clock was ticking since he'd be leaving the Rocking C after the party.

"I planned to call the Hoffmans later today," Lainie added. "So I'll ask if they have any concerns about the kids having a hayride, although I don't think they will."

She clearly didn't want to address their undeniable attraction, the heated kiss they'd just shared or where it might lead. He should leave it at that, right?

"While I'm on the phone, I should probably lock in a time for the party. How do you feel about two o'clock? Or should we include the children for lunch?" She bit down on her bottom lip again, but this time, when she looked up, her eyes glistened like warm honey. "There's so much I want to do."

"You're really excited about this party, aren't you?"

"More than you know." She ran a hand through her hair, which had gotten mussed with the tumble and the kiss. Her fingers caught on a tangle, and she tugged through it. "But it's not just about this particular party.

After Christmas, I'm going to stay in close contact with the Hoffmans and do everything I can to support Kidville. My heart's gone out to those kids, especially Andre."

Drew felt the same way. "I'd like to continue helping them, too. I mean personally and not only through Esteban Enterprises."

"Jim and Donna will be happy to hear that. They're going to need all the support and manpower they can get." Again, she pointed to the buckboard. "And speaking of manpower, who's going to refurbish this wagon and make sure it's safe to carry the kids? And where do we get the straw?"

"I'll take care of it. And I'll rope Sully and Rex into helping me. It'll be good for them to have a job to do and something to look forward to."

Lainie smiled. "That reminds me, I need to get back to the kitchen, or lunch won't be on the table by noon." Then she turned and walked away as if nothing had happened, as if they'd never kissed.

Drew studied her from behind, watching the sway of her denim-clad hips and the way that flannel shirt ruffled in the light afternoon breeze. He felt badly about feeling her up, especially if that's what had unsettled her. But he'd felt compelled to learn what she was hiding underneath her unflattering fabric façade.

And if things worked out the way he hoped they would, one day soon he'd find out.

Lainie hurried toward the house, determined to escape Drew and the powerful yet unsettling feelings he stirred up inside her. But now that she'd kissed him and experienced his heated touch, she doubted her efforts would work.

He'd set her soul on fire, and as he'd caressed her, she'd nearly melted into a puddle on the grass. His touch created an ache deep in her core, and she'd nearly forgotten she had a physical flaw.

But when his hand moved dangerously close to her chest, she'd suddenly realized that he was just one tantalizing stroke away from stumbling upon her scar. And she'd freaked out like a feral cat. How embarrassing was that?

If things progressed between them, if they became lovers—and if truth be told, she wasn't opposed to that any longer—she'd tell him about the surgery and prepare him for what he was about to see. The last thing she wanted was for him to be repulsed, just as Ryan had been when he'd frozen up and turned a romantic moment ugly.

But then again, Drew seemed to be different from Ryan—and certainly from Craig. Could she risk being completely honest with him?

She was healthy and whole now. Besides, it might not matter to Drew that she bore a hardened ridge and a pale white line that would never go away.

At the possibility that he might accept her completely, an idea sparked and a new game plan arose.

She'd start looking like herself again. First step: wearing lipstick instead of the gloss she'd applied earlier. And she'd choose clothes that were more feminine, more stylish. More flattering. Then, when the subject came up again, and the timing was right, she'd level with him about her surgery.

By the time she opened the back door and entered the house, she felt much better and a lot more confident. And when she spotted Sully seated at the table, she burst into a smile.

"There you are," her old friend said. "I've been looking for you."

Thank goodness he hadn't gone in search of her behind the barn!

"I went with Drew to see the wagon he'd like to use for the hayride," she said. "Is everything okay?"

"Everything's hunky-dory. I just wanted to share some good news."

"What's up?"

Sully leaned back in his seat, clasped his hands and rested them on his rounded belly. "A few years back, I used to be a member of the Brighton Valley Moose Lodge. Every December they'd have a holiday party, and Santa Claus always made a showing. So I called an old friend who's still active with the group and asked if I could borrow their suit after they finish with it."

"What'd he say?"

"They'll loan it to us. And after I told him why we needed it, he offered to have it dry cleaned and promised to deliver it himself." Sully grinned from ear to ear, clearly pleased with his contribution to the party.

"That's great," Lainie said. "Things are coming together nicely. Getting a Santa suit is one thing I can mark off my list, but there's still a lot to do."

"Let me know if there's anything else I can do to help."

"Thanks, I'll keep that in mind." She'd also have to remember to place that phone call to Kidville. She didn't want to make any more plans before talking things over with the Hoffmans first.

After Sully left the kitchen, Lainie glanced at the clock over the stove. She'd better get the chicken in the oven or it wouldn't be ready by noon.

Ten minutes later, using the old-style phone that hung on the kitchen wall, she placed the call to Kidville.

When Donna answered, Lainie launched into their party plans, including the hayride that would wrap up the day. Just as expected, Donna gave her full approval, and they settled on a one o'clock start time.

"There's something else I had on my mind," Lainie said. "We offered Andre a horseback ride, and Drew found the perfect horse for him, a gentle mare named Felicity. Would it be all right if Andre came to the Rocking C for a lesson within the next few days?"

"That would be awesome. He seems to be adjusting pretty well to being here with us, but he's still very concerned about his little brothers. Maybe visiting the ranch and riding a horse will help him take his mind off his worries, at least for an hour or two."

"Are the younger boys together in the same foster home?" Lainie asked.

"I wish they were. Sadly, there are more children in the county who need a place to live than families willing to take them in. But Mrs. Tran, their social worker, believes siblings should be together whenever possible. So I hope and pray they won't have to be separated too long."

Lainie's heart clenched, and her grip on the telephone receiver tightened. "Are the children adoptable?"

"I expect the youngest boys to be cleared soon. Their father is serving a life sentence without possibility of parole. And from what I understand, he's going to surrender parental rights, which would make Abel and Mario eligible for adoption."

"But what about Andre?" Lainie's grip on the receiver tightened until her knuckles ached.

"I'm not sure. His father ran off years ago, and no one knows where he is. On top of that, the poor kid is facing several surgeries and some extensive rehab, so he's in limbo. At least, legally. Jim and I are doing all we can to make him feel loved and safe."

Lainie had no doubt about that, but still…

"I'd take all three boys in a heartbeat," she said, "if that meant they could stay together. But I'm not prepared to provide them with a permanent home just yet."

"That's sweet of you to even consider it," Donna said.

Lainie wasn't just blowing smoke and offering something she didn't expect to follow through on. It had been a heartfelt offer, and she wanted to make sure Donna realized it.

"I'm serious," Lainie said. "I'd have to do some footwork first. I have a small apartment in town, so I'd need to find a bigger place." Not to mention a better-paying job.

Then again, if Lainie went to work full-time to support a family, she'd need day care for the kids. And that wouldn't allow her to give them all the time and affection they needed—and deserved.

Or would it? A lot of single parents had to work, yet they still found a way to spend quality time with their kids.

"Would the state allow me to adopt as a single woman? Or at least, become a foster mother?"

"I can place a call to Mrs. Tran and ask," Donna said. "Or better yet, I can give you her number."

Lainie sucked in a deep breath, then let out a wobbly sigh. "My position at the Rocking C is only temporary, so I'd need to find a different job first. Maybe it would be best if I called Mrs. Tran after I get settled."

The more she thought about it, the more the idea sounded like a pipe dream that couldn't possibly come true. By the time she was capable of providing those children with a home, Mrs. Tran might have found a better living situation for all of them. Or by then, Kidville would be able to expand and accept younger children.

Hopefully, Andre's little brothers were in loving environments and would have a nice Christmas this year, even if they…

"Say," Lainie said, "could we invite Andre's brothers to the party? We'd include their foster families, too, of course."

"That's a great idea, and I know Andre would be thrilled if they came. I'll call Mrs. Tran and see what she has to say. It might be difficult to coordinate something like that on Christmas Eve since everyone could have different holiday plans. But it might work. In the meantime, when did you want to schedule that riding lesson for Andre?"

"As soon as possible."

"I'm happy to hear that," Donna said. "That little boy has had to face a lot of broken promises in the past."

Lainie could certainly relate to that. The two men she'd once cared about had been big disappointments, too.

But then she'd met Drew. Hopefully, if she were to consider having a relationship with him, it would prove to be a lot more promising than the other two.

Drew stood on the front porch, drinking a cup of coffee and waiting for Jim Hoffman to bring Andre for his riding lesson. The morning air was crisp—not exactly cold, but chilly enough to know winter had crept in on them.

When the screen door creaked open, Lainie stepped outside with a plastic container in her hand. He'd already seen her at breakfast this morning and noted the change in her. She'd ditched the baggy denim for a pair of snug black jeans and a stylish, curve-hugging sweater. She'd even applied lipstick.

But seeing her now, without the full-length apron to cover her up, he realized he was going to have a hell of a time keeping his eyes off her and focused on Andre and his riding lesson.

"What have you got there?" he asked.

"Just a couple of carrots and an apple. I thought Andre could give them to Felicity before or after his ride. But I thought I'd better ask you first." She glanced out to the corral, where Felicity was saddled and tied to a hitching post. "Is that her?"

"She isn't used to getting much special attention, so she'll like having a treat."

"Sounds like she and Andre have something in common," Lainie said.

Drew was getting some special treatment today, too. Not only was Lainie a lovely eyeful, she was wearing a new fragrance, something soft and tropical, which seemed out of place at a ranch. Actually, now that she'd ditched the baggy denim and blousy cotton, she seemed out of place here, too.

He'd found her attractive before, but today, she was beautiful and downright sexy.

From what he'd seen so far, it appeared that she had a good heart, and an unusual thought struck him, one that was a little too domestic for a man who'd made up his mind to remain single the rest of his life.

That decision had been fairly easy to make, when the people who should have loved and supported him as a kid had all failed him one way or another—whether through sickness or desertion.

Okay. So Kara had never let him down, but that was different. She wasn't supposed to look after him. It was the other way around.

"Come on." Drew gave Lainie a gentle nudge with his elbow. "I'll introduce you to Felicity."

They'd just stepped off the porch when a white mini-van pulled into the yard.

"Oh, good," Lainie said. "Andre's here."

The moment Jim and the boy climbed out of the vehicle, Andre broke into a happy grin.

"I've never been on a ranch before." His small brown eyes glowed with excitement. "I didn't think today would ever get here."

"That's true," Jim said. "He hardly got a wink of sleep last night, and he's been jabbering nonstop about cowboys and horses ever since we told him about the riding lesson."

"I'm glad we can provide a little fun for him," Drew said.

"So am I." Jim placed his hand on the boy's small shoulder. "I'd love to stay in the yard and watch you guys, but I'm taking a new medication for the next week or so, and I'm supposed to stay out of the direct sunlight."

"Why don't you sit on the porch," Drew said. "I have a feeling several of the retired cowboys will soon join you. They like sitting in those rockers in the shade."

"Great. I'd like to meet them." Jim placed his hand on the pint-size, wannabe cowboy's head. "Have fun, Andre." Then he turned and headed toward the porch.

"This is so cool." Andre scanned the pastures, the corral and the barn. "I wish Abel and Mario could be here to see this."

Drew glanced at Lainie, whose glassy eyes revealed her sympathy. Rather than stir up any sadness—hers or Andre's—he decided to let the boy's comment ride.

But Lainie faced it head-on. "I'll try to set up a visit for your brothers to come to the Rocking C, too."

Why had she offered something she might not be able to pull off? If it didn't work out for any reason, it would only make the poor kid feel worse.

"That'd be awesome." Andre looked up at Lainie as if she held all power, all knowledge… All hope. "Can I come again when they get their lesson?"

"Of course you can. They won't have as much fun without you."

There she went again, committing Drew to something without running it by him first.

Of course, she hadn't actually included him in her plan, but she wasn't going to be living on the ranch much longer. How did she think she'd find time to set up another visit with two separate families?

"Andre," she said, as she stooped to tie the boy's shoes, "tell me about your brothers. I can't wait to meet them."

Aw, man. Why'd she have to go and do that? The poor kid didn't need those sad, painful feelings stirred up. He needed to learn to tamp them down. If Drew had allowed himself to get sucked into the emotions his mom and sister had once faced, he wouldn't have been able to stay strong for them.

"Mario is four," Andre said, "and Abel is six. They have a different dad than me, and I'm glad about that because he's in prison." Andre glanced down at his sneakers, which were now double knotted, then back at Lainie. "I never met my dad, but my mom told me he was a cowboy. And the best one ever. So when I grow up, I wanna be just like him."

Drew's gut twisted at the thought that Andre's dead-beat dad had become a superhero, a mythical cowboy who'd bailed out on his own flesh and blood, just like Drew's old man had done.

"Do you have any idea where your father might be?" Lainie asked.

"No, but he's probably working on a ranch like this one. He's a nice man, and not like Pete. My dad would never hurt a kid or a mom."

At that, Drew's hand fisted, and his heart clenched so hard it almost choked off his air supply.

He wasn't about to stand here and let Lainie resurrect the past, ruining the boy's day—and possibly his future. So he had to put a stop to it here and now.

"Come on," he told Andre. "I've got a hat for you in the barn. Once you're dressed like a real cowboy, I'll introduce you to Felicity, the mare you're going to ride."

"Cool," the boy said, as he limped along with Drew. "I can't wait to ride her."

When he and Andre returned from the barn, Lainie was waiting for them inside the corral and next to the mare.

"You look like a real cowboy." She tapped the top of his new hat. "Now let's see how you look mounted on Felicity."

Apparently she intended to stick around and witness the boy's first ride, which was okay with Drew.

He liked having her around—at least, as long as she didn't pry or poke at tender feelings.

As Drew walked toward the gate, Andre limping along beside him, Lainie lifted the plastic container. "I brought this so you could give Felicity a treat before you ride her. I have an apple and two carrots. Which do you want to give her?"

Andre looked at Drew. "Which one would she like best?"

"Let's give it all to her." Drew reached into his pocket, pulled out a Swiss Army knife his sister had given him last Christmas and cut the apple into chunks.

"Is it bad for her to eat big pieces?" Andre asked.

"No, but she'll gobble it up so fast she won't get a chance to taste it. Let's make her work for it." He handed a chunk of apple to Andre, then showed him how to keep his hand open flat while he offered it to her.

Just like the cowboy he wanted to be, Andre took to feeding a horse quickly. All the while, he beamed and giggled.

Felicity seemed to take a real liking to him, too.

"Let's get you in that saddle," Drew said, "so we can start your riding lesson."

Minutes later, as Drew adjusted the stirrups, he glanced up and caught the happy smile on Andre's face. His chest filled with warmth, just knowing he'd had a part in putting it there.

The lesson began, and Andre was a natural. Before long, Drew was able to step back and let the horse and boy move about the corral.

As he leaned against one of the posts, Lainie stood next to him, only the white wooden railing separating them.

"Look at him," Drew said. "He's having the time of his life."

"You're good at this," Lainie said.

At what? Surely she didn't mean he was good with kids. His expertise was horses, although he had to admit to having a soft spot for a disabled kid who wanted to grow up to be a cowboy. But he thanked her just the same.

Then he looked over his shoulder, caught her profile, the thick dark lashes, lengthened by mascara. The turned-up nose. The fresh application of dark pink lipstick.

"You look pretty today," he said.

"Thank you."

"What's the big occasion?"

She shrugged a single shoulder. "I just wanted to look nice for Andre's big ride."

"Then it worked."

Her smile reached her eyes, sparking a glow that made the color look amber.

"Those black jeans are a lot more flattering than overalls," he said, wondering what style panties she wore today. Were they pink and lacy like before? Or maybe satin like the soft bra he'd touched the other day?

He didn't ask, and she didn't comment further. Instead, he checked on Andre, who had a steady grip on the reins. The kid was a quick study, which was good since Drew couldn't keep his mind or his eyes off Lainie.

Maybe it was her scent, which reminded him of a big, frozen piña colada, complete with a slice of fresh pineapple.

She was pretty damned tempting—sweet and intoxicating. What he wouldn't give to get her alone. To see if she tasted as good as she smelled.

He really didn't know that much about her, though. But since he didn't make long-term commitments, did that even matter?

The next time he had a moment alone with her, he just might suggest they have an affair while they were both here.

That reminded him, time was slipping away.

"Are you still planning to edit my blog posts?" he asked.

"Sure. Have you started it yet?"

"I wrote about one of the cowboys, but it's still in draft form and needs work. I thought that you might want to look it over and tell me what you think. It'd be nice to know if I'm heading in the right direction."

"I'd be happy to." She offered him another smile, and he was again struck by her beauty. And by the appeal of a romantic distraction until Christmas.

"I've got some things to do in the kitchen," she said. "So this isn't a good time to see what you've pulled together. What about after dinner tonight?"

Bedtime? He liked the sound of that.

"Perfect," he said. "I'll have my laptop all set up.

Once you think the first blog post is ready to go, I'll schedule it and start work on the second one."

"I'm looking forward to it," she said.

So was he. Hopefully, she'd be agreeable to love-making. Only trouble was, they'd both be moving on and going their own ways soon. So he'd better suggest it tonight.

Chapter Ten

Lainie could hardly wait to finish her evening chores, slip away from the house and head to the cabin where Drew was staying. And she suspected that he felt that same eagerness.

Several times during dinner she'd caught him gazing at her so intensely that it seemed as if he was looking beyond her outward appearance and into her very heart and soul. It had been a little unraveling, but in a good way.

He didn't know about the scar yet, but she planned to tell him about it tonight.

She ought to be nervous about that, but she wasn't. She'd come to realize Drew was special. A flood of warmth had filled her chest when she saw him with Andre today, when she'd observed the kindness he'd shown, the sensitivity. She'd nearly melted when she'd watched him slow his steps so the limping boy could keep up with him.

And that's when she'd lowered her guard and finally faced what she was really feeling for him.

They would work on his blog tonight, but they'd also have a heart-to-heart talk. No more secrets. No surprises.

Besides, Lainie's congenital heart defect had been corrected years ago. And that scar was her badge of courage, as one of the nurses in the pediatric intensive care unit had told her.

She'd have to tap into that bravery while she waited for his reaction to her revelation like a timid little girl being wheeled into the operating room to face the unknown. Would he accept or reject her?

Shame on him if he didn't, yet her heart swelled with hope. She'd come to care deeply for Drew. She might even love him. At least, that's what she'd imagined love might feel like. And if he gave her any reason to believe he felt the same way, she'd come out and tell him to his face.

Once Lainie had washed the dishes and put them away, she blew out a ragged sigh, then glanced at the clock on the wall, ticking out the minutes until she could see him again. It was nearing showtime. So she returned to her bedroom to freshen up—and pull out all the stops.

As she stood in front of the bathroom mirror, she ran a brush through her hair and let the curls tumble down her shoulders the way they used to. She'd gotten tired of hiding her looks, her identity.

Heck, she might even tell him about that fiasco with Craig. That way, in case he ever heard about it, he'd know the truth.

After reapplying her lipstick and mascara, she used a little blush, although she probably wouldn't need it. Excitement and nervous anticipation were sure to paint her cheeks a warm, rosy hue.

Before leaving for Drew's cabin, she took one last look in the mirror. She wanted to put her best foot forward before knocking on his door tonight.

Pleased by the familiar image looking back at her, she said, "This is it."

Now was the time to let Drew know who she really was. And to find out if he would accept the real Lainie.

After eating dinner in the kitchen with the ranch hands, Drew returned to his cabin to get ready for Lainie. He was excited about her visit—and not just because he wanted her help on writing up his interviews.

Something told him that tonight was going to be special, and that he should be prepared for anything. So he'd taken a shower, slipped into a clean pair of worn jeans and put on a Texas A & M polo shirt. Once an Aggie, always an Aggie. Right?

His hair was still damp when he sat down at the dinette table, his makeshift home office, and booted up his laptop. He may as well set the scene so Lainie would think that work was the only thing he had on his mind, but his hormones had already caused his thoughts to stray in a sexual direction.

He wished he could offer her a glass of wine or a cold bottle of beer. All he had to drink was coffee or soda pop, which would have to do. But an adult beverage would be a lot more conducive to romance.

Then again, so was a sugar cookie.

And a broken tailgate.

He'd just logged on to the internet when an on-line call from his sister came through. The last time they'd talked, Kara had insisted that she was doing well. Hopefully, that was still the case.

"Hey," he said, once they connected. "What's up?"

"Not much. Just the same old, same old. But I'm hanging in there."

He could see her stretched out on her bed, where several big, fluffy pillows propped up her head. She appeared to be a little pale, but maybe it was just the lighting.

"When's your next doctor visit?" he asked.

"I see her on Monday. Since I've made it another week, she might let me start moving around again."

"I don't blame you for wanting to get out of bed. You've been housebound for so long."

"Yeah, I know. Who'd think going to an obstetrical visit would be something to celebrate?"

He laughed. "Not me. How's that woman I hired to help you working out?"

"She's great. She sits with me during the day and keeps me company. We're watching entire seasons of *Downton Abbey*."

Drew'd pass on that. "And how's her cooking?"

"The best mac and cheese this side of the Mississippi."

"Don't get fat."

She patted her tummy. "Ha, ha." Then her expression turned a little more serious. "How's life on the Rocking Chair Ranch?"

"Not bad. A couple of the retired cowboys are a real hoot. And all of them are pretty cool, with interesting pasts."

"Have you started writing the blog?"

"Yeah, but it's still just a draft. I've asked a woman who lives here to edit them for me."

Kara readjusted herself in bed. "Who is she?"

"Her name is Lainie. She's filling in temporarily for the ranch cook. She's a nice woman, and she's talked me into helping her plan a Christmas party."

"Hmm." A slow smile stretched across Kara's lips, providing a little color to her face. "Do I sense a little romance in the air?"

A zing hit his stomach. "No, but I have to admit, the thought has crossed my mind." Drew glanced at the clock on the microwave. Maybe he ought to end his call before Lainie arrived. His sister was more than a little nosy and could be pushy at times.

Then again, he could always introduce them. What would it hurt?

He was still pondering a decision when a knock sounded at the door. He didn't have to open it to know who'd arrived.

Aw, what the heck. Why not?

"Hang on, Kara. She's here now."

"Ooh. You mean I get to meet her? That's cool. You usually keep the women you date at a distance."

"Just from you." He scooted his chair back and got to his feet. "And just so you know, we're not dating. Not yet, anyway."

He heard Kara laugh in the background as he answered the door and let Lainie inside.

Damn, she looked good tonight. She was dressed to kill in a pair of sleek black slacks and a white blouse. And that hair? A man could get lost in soft, flowing curls like that. She'd freshened her lipstick, too. Red this time.

Clearly, Drew wasn't the only one who had romance on the mind, and it took every ounce of self-control not to welcome her with a heartfelt, hormone-driven kiss.

"Are you going to invite me in?" she asked.

"Sorry. Of course." His tongue tripped over the words, and he stepped aside.

Again, he regretted that he didn't have anything to offer her stronger than root beer or an after-the-lovin' midnight snack.

As they crossed the small living area to the laptop, he said, "You're just in time to meet my sister."

Lainie scanned the interior of the tiny cabin, which was obviously empty, and her brow creased.

"She's not actually *here*. She's online—I'm talking to her now." He led her to the laptop, where his sister waited on the screen. A smile tugged at his lips. Kara had been right. He'd always kept his relationships private and hadn't introduced her to any of his lovers in the past. But Lainie was different. Maybe he did have a domestic side he'd kept hidden.

"Kara," he said, waiting to witness their first inter-action. "This is Lainie."

Drew wasn't sure what he'd expected, but certainly not his sister's strangled gasp.

He shot a glance at Lainie, who'd slapped her hand to her throat and recoiled as if she'd just spotted an-other mouse in the cabin. No, worse than that.

"What in the hell is *she* doing with you?" Kara asked.

Drew didn't understand. He glanced first at his star-tled sister on the screen, then at Lainie, her eyes wide, the color fading from her face.

"I'm sorry," Lainie said. "I had no idea…"

"About what?" Drew was at a loss. What was hap-pening?

He looked back at the screen to see Kara sitting up in bed, no longer resting her head on a pile of pillows, her finger raised and shaking. "Oh, my God, Drew. I don't believe it. You're dating the woman who broke up my marriage."

"Lainie? No way." He'd seen the brunette in question— or rather, her image when that bar scene video had gone viral. Her hair was the same color, and her curls bounced along her shoulders when she strode away from the res-taurant confrontation in a huff.

But now that he thought about it, their faces *were* similar. Especially with Lainie's red lipstick.

"I have no idea what's going on," Drew told his sister. "But I'll get to the bottom of this. And when I do, I'll call you back."

Drew disconnected the call, turned to Lainie and folded his arms across his chest. "I don't understand. Who are you? And what's my sister talking about?"

"I can explain," Lainie said. "I did date Craig, but not very long. And just so you know, I haven't seen him since that awful day at the hotel."

Dammit. "You're Elena?"

"Yes, but I can explain."

No wonder she'd seemed familiar to him. And now he was looking at the woman who'd slept with Craig, destroyed his and Kara Lee's marriage and nearly caused his sister to lose her baby. Apparently, he'd been wrong about Lainie or Elena or whatever her name really was.

"Go ahead." His eyes narrowed. "I'm listening."

"I had no idea Craig was married," she said. "I didn't even know who he was—I don't follow the rodeo circuit. He lied to me and led me on."

Drew's stomach twisted into a knot. Craig was an ass, that's for sure. But the whole idea sickened him. Damn. He'd almost gotten involved with a woman his ex-brother-in-law had slept with.

And worse, just seeing Lainie at the cabin with Drew was going to kill his sister. Hell, it was bothering the crap out of him just to think about it.

"Don't look at me like that," Lainie said. "There's no way I would have gone out with Craig if I'd known he was married."

"I can't buy that. How could a journalist be so naïve? That is, if you actually *are* a journalist."

"Now that—" she stabbed her finger at him "—is insulting."

"You can't be a very good one if you didn't figure out Craig was married. He's not a hermit. And practically everyone on the circuit knows Kara."

She sucked in a breath. "I screwed up. Okay? I'm human."

And one who was sexier than he'd ever seen her before. Just look at her all dolled up. Had she planned to come on to him tonight? And if so, for what purpose?

He raked his hand through his damp hair, stymied. Perplexed. Pissed.

"Apparently, you believe the worst about me," Lainie said.

He didn't want to. But maybe it was easier that way, to get angry and cut his losses before she inflicted even more pain on his family. Besides, he couldn't very well choose between Lainie and Kara. And he damn sure couldn't sleep with his ex-brother-in-law's lover.

"Believe it or not," Lainie said, "your sister wasn't the only victim in all of this."

Maybe so, but the only victim who really mattered right now was Kara.

"You should leave," Drew said.

"No. Talk to me."

How could he? "You've put me in an awkward position." And an impossible one, it seemed. "Tell me something. Did you know Craig was my brother-in-law?"

"No, of course not. Do you think I'm scheming you or something?"

"Either that, or again, you're a lousy journalist. If you had even an ounce of investigative chops, you would have found out about my family."

Her expression went from angry to hurt, and she threw up her hands. "I give up. It isn't worth it." Then she turned on her heel and headed for the cabin door. Before reaching for the knob, she paused and turned back to him. "I hope your anger at me won't stop you from helping Andre and the other children at Kidville."

"I wouldn't do that," he said. "I intend to follow through on my commitment to get financial support for those kids."

"That's a relief. And for the record, I plan to make that Christmas party special—with or without your help. Those kids have had too many disappointments in life."

She gave him only a beat to answer, but a flurry of emotion balled up in his throat, making it hard to speak, even if he could have found the words to say.

Then she let herself out, the door clicking shut behind her, severing what little connection they'd once had.

Drew flopped onto his bed and scrubbed his hands over his face. He should be relieved that she was gone, but an ache settled deep in his chest. Now what? He'd always been a fixer, but he didn't have a clue how to clean up this mess.

A hodgepodge of emotion swirled around his heart like a Texas twister. Regret that his sister had been hurt. Disappointment that Lainie wasn't the woman he'd thought she was. And worse yet, fear that she actually was that woman and that he couldn't pursue her now. Not after she'd slept with Craig and had been involved in his sister's divorce.

But he wouldn't try to sort through his tangled up feelings when he had a phone call to make and a sister to calm. The last thing he needed right now was for Kara to go into premature labor again.

Tears streamed down Lainie's cheeks as she marched across the yard and away from the cabin, but she was too crushed and disappointed to swipe them away. She'd been let down yet again by a man she'd once cared about. Only this time, it was different—worse. She'd allowed herself to become way too invested in Drew, when she should have known better than to take that risk.

On top of that, she was angry as hell. He'd not only considered her a floozy and a liar, which was bad enough, but he'd accused her of being a lousy journalist, the one thing she had pride in.

Sure, she should have done a background check on Craig. And on Kara. Heck, she should have done one on Drew, too. But was she supposed to dig into the lives of everyone she met?

"Ooh!" She had to walk off some of the built-up steam before entering the house. She circled the outside of the empty corral, trying to shake off her grief and come to grips with her emotions.

Drew had assumed the worst about her and wouldn't

let her explain. Gosh, you'd think he'd at least listen to her side of the story. After all they'd done together—the long talks, the visit to Kidville, the Christmas plans they'd made…

And what about the amazing kisses they'd shared?

Darn it. She'd actually begun to care about him, to believe he was different, that he was worth her affection. Given time, she might have fallen in love with him.

But who was she kidding? Her feelings for him bordered on love already, if she hadn't actually taken a hard tumble into a romantic abyss.

Her heart ached, but as she circled the corral a second time, hurt gave way to anger. She wanted to lash out at someone. Anyone.

It was almost funny, though. In the past, she might have gone undercover or run away, like she'd done after that horrible confrontation with Craig's wife—or rather, Drew's sister—at the Houston hotel restaurant.

But Lainie wasn't about to slip into old habits. She might have had a lousy childhood and faced some difficult hurdles, but she'd come a long way since then. That, in itself, demanded that she hold her head high from now on.

She was Elena "Lainie" Montoya, up-and-coming journalist. She was also "Dear Debbie" to Mr. Carlton. And from this day forward, she didn't give a rip who knew her true identity or what she stood for.

And she'd no longer struggle with her outward appearance, either. She liked what she saw in the mirror and would embrace it, whether she chose to wear denim or silk, overalls or stilettos.

Lainie had a *lot* going for her. She was a recent college graduate with a bright, shiny future ahead of her. Someday she'd be an investigative reporter who would change the world, one story at a time.

Tired of circling the corral, she headed toward the barn. She paused near the buckboard, which was barely visible in the darkened yard. Her heart clenched as she looked at the grassy ground, where she'd been so swayed by Drew's kiss that she'd nearly convinced herself that he was the guy she'd been waiting for all of her life. And that they could have something special together, but she'd better forget that crazy idea.

One day soon, she'd have it all—a successful career, a family of her own *and* a loving husband. She just hadn't met him yet.

Feeling much better and back in control of her thoughts and emotions, she turned toward the house, but she wouldn't go inside just yet. She wanted more time to suck in the cold ranch air, to remain in the shadows and form a game plan from this night forward.

She'd hardly taken a single breath when the mudroom door swung open, and Sully walked out.

"There you are," Sully said. "I wondered where you ran off to."

Lainie continued to stand outside the ring of the porch light, where Sully couldn't detect any lingering moisture on her face.

"I just wanted a little fresh air and exercise," she said. "Did you need to talk to me?"

"Only to tell you I'm going to Tennessee, but I plan to be back for the Christmas party."

"Seriously?" Panic at the unexpected announcement laced her voice. "Why?"

"My brother's in the hospital."

"I'm so sorry to hear that. What's wrong?"

"His ticker is giving him grief, but the doctors say he's going to be okay. He wants to move to the Rocking Chair Ranch as soon as he's discharged, but his family isn't onboard. I plan to talk to them on his behalf, and then I'll bring him back with me."

"How long will you be gone?"

"A few days. You gonna miss me, sweetie?"

"Of course I will." And on many levels. Lainie certainly understood why Sully had to go, but her next column was due before he could possibly return. "When are you leaving?"

"First thing in the morning. And way before breakfast, so I thought I'd better tell you goodbye now."

How in the world was she going to be able to offer advice to the lovelorn without the wise old man's help?

Worse yet, who was she going to confide in about her own heartache and disappointment?

"You look worried," Sully said.

"Just about the party," she lied. "The kids will be disappointed if Santa isn't here."

"Don't worry, Lainie. I'll be back at least three days before the party. You can count on me."

Apparently, Sully was the only man she could count on, so she eased into the light emanating from the porch, swiping her eyes with the back of her hand and forcing a carefree grin.

As she continued forward to offer Sully a goodbye hug, he squinted and crunched his craggy brow. "Don't you look pretty tonight. But are you crying?"

"No, I had something in my eye."

"That better be all it is, because if one of those cowboys around here has hurt your feelings or toyed with your heart, he'll hear from me."

"Just a piece of straw or an eyelash. But it's out now." She embraced her sweet old friend, breathing in the faint scent of laundry soap on his green flannel shirt and catching a whiff of chocolate. "Did you get into the leftover brownies for another bedtime snack?"

"Don't tell the nurses," he said. "They think I'm getting fat."

If Lainie's heart hadn't been so heavy, she might have laughed. Instead she smiled. "I won't say a word about you raiding the kitchen to appease your sweet tooth. At least, not until after the party. I wouldn't want the kids to see a skinny Santa."

"No worries about that." Sully chuckled. "And just so you know, I've been practicing. How's this? *Ho, ho, ho! Merry Christmas.*"

At that, Lainie did laugh. "It's perfect." Then she followed him into the house.

"I'd better turn in," he said. "It'll be time for me to head for the airport before you know it."

And it would be time for Lainie to turn in that blasted column before she knew it, too.

Once inside her bedroom, she was tempted to crawl

into bed and forget about her deadline until tomorrow. But the sooner she took a look at the latest batch of letters, the better off she'd be.

Interestingly enough, and right off the bat, she spotted a problem she could respond to.

Dear Debbie,

I'm so upset with my sister (I'll call her Connie) that I can hardly see straight. We had a crappy childhood and grew up in a dysfunctional home. Since we only had each other, we've always been very close. But recently, Connie started dating this guy (I'll call him Mike). I told Connie I didn't like him, but she didn't care. Now she spends every waking hour with him and doesn't have time to go to lunch or a movie with me. We don't even talk on the phone anymore.

Last night, Connie came home with an engagement ring. She announced that she was going to marry him in a couple of months and asked me to be her bridesmaid. I told her that was way too soon. She needs to get to know Mike better. I mean, he's still in college and works as a barista at a local coffee place. So it's not like she's marrying a guy who can support her the minute they say "I do."

We argued, and things got ugly. I refused to attend her wedding, so she told me she'd ask Mike's sister to stand up with her. How's that for loyalty?

I'm tempted to disown her—or whatever it is

*siblings do when they don't want to be related
anymore. But I'm not quite ready to do that. At
least, not yet.*

*So here's my question, Dear Debbie: How do
I talk her out of marrying a guy she's only known
for three months? That's not enough time for her
to find out if he's going to turn out to be a mean
drunk like our father was. I'm only trying to protect her, but Connie doesn't see it that way. How
do I convince her she's wrong?*
Brokenhearted Sister

An answer came to Lainie right away, so she
cranked up her laptop and got to work. The words
flowed easily, and her advice was heartfelt and sound.

Apparently, she'd learned a lot from talking to
Sully in the past, from listening to the way he rea-
soned things out.

For the first time, she'd responded to the writer as
Elena Montoya, sharing things she'd never told anyone.
She knew a thing or two about being hurt, about having
people betray her. And, sadly, about betraying people
herself, even if it had been completely unintentional.

But it felt good be authentic. To give advice from
her heart. She just wished she'd been authentic with
Drew, too.

Or course, it was too late for that. And maybe that
was just as well. It was one thing sharing her heart and
soul to a stranger and under the guise of Dear Debbie,
and it was another to reopen old wounds and lay herself
open and vulnerable to a man who'd broken her heart.

After shutting down her laptop, she walked over to the bedroom window and peered out into the night. She didn't expect to see Drew's cabin in the dark, but with the inside lights blazing, she spotted it right away.

Was he still awake? Was he working on the blog?

Or was he, like Lainie, mulling over what they might have had and lost?

Chapter Eleven

It was nearing midnight, but Drew wasn't ready for bed or even close to falling asleep. Just a couple of hours ago, he'd called Kara and told her to think about the baby. He'd reminded her that her tiny son needed a peaceful environment in which he could grow, and that's all it had taken to convince her to calm her down.

On the other hand, Drew was still wound up tighter than a guitar string ready to snap. He couldn't get over the revelation that Lainie had been Craig's lover.

Now, as he paced the floor of the small cabin like a caged mountain lion, he wished he could relax. He probably ought to use his time wisely by working on his blog, but the only thing he could focus on was Lainie.

Who was the woman who'd nearly stolen his heart? Angel or vixen?

He wished he knew. His gut told him she wasn't the type to intentionally date a married man. He'd always been a good judge of character. Shouldn't he trust his instinct when it came to Lainie?

Then again, she had a deceptive side, a major flaw he'd failed to see. Even Sully had pointed it out.

I guess everyone has a weakness, the old man had said.

It seems that one of her girlfriends or someone she knows has a problem, usually due to their own making. Then he'd added, *Lainie really needs to choose some new friends. Some of them don't have the sense the Good Lord gave a goose.*

Drew hadn't met any of her friends, and after what Sully had told him about them, he hadn't wanted to.

Still, if she had some loser friends, was that a bad sign? Or was it the result of having a naïve and loving heart?

She was good with the old cowboys—and with kids like Andre. Didn't that prove she was kind and thoughtful? But then again, was that just an act?

There'd been other incidents and comments made that might've offered him a clue. Like the day she'd touched his forearm and dazzled him with a pretty smile. *You'll help me, won't you? You said you'd do anything that needed to be done.* She'd practically batted her eyelashes, working her wiles on him.

He'd failed to pick up on the possibility that she might've been playing him. Instead, when she'd zapped his nerve endings with her touch and gazed at him sweetly, he'd been captivated and completely swayed.

Sure, helping her plan a Christmas party for the children wasn't a bad thing. But that wasn't the point. Hadn't she just blurted out the idea, committing him to help before asking him first?

Then there was that sexually charged embrace near the barn earlier today. She'd been kissing him back like there was no tomorrow, when all of a sudden she'd torn her mouth from his and pushed him away as if he'd been a real horn dog. Yet just a heartbeat before, she'd made it pretty clear that she wouldn't mind if he'd taken her right there, in the soft grass and under cover of an old buckboard.

I didn't mean to overreact, she'd said. *Or to be a tease.*

He'd accepted her response at face value, but now he couldn't help wondering if she'd known exactly what she'd been doing.

Had she played on Craig's attraction to her in that same way?

Drew didn't want to believe so, but he supposed it was possible. Hadn't Lainie taken to wearing makeup recently? Was that an attempt to draw Drew deeper under her spell?

There lay the crux of his problem. He couldn't figure her out.

Even if she was as goodhearted as he'd once thought she was and Craig had duped her, like he had so many other people, Drew would still have to give her up for good. How could he date her knowing how his sister felt about her? Besides, no matter what the circumstances had been, she'd also slept with Craig.

Wasn't it easier—and safer—to believe the worst?

Drew blew out a ragged breath. More than two hours had passed since their online showdown, and he still wasn't anywhere near a decision or a judgment. He stopped pacing and glanced at the bed. He really ought to turn in for the night, but his thoughts kept tumbling and rumbling through his brain, making it impossible to rest.

Damn. He'd probably be up until dawn, stewing about Elena.

And ruing the fact that he'd never kiss "Lainie" again.

Much to Lainie's surprise, Drew hadn't avoided her. He showed up in the kitchen for breakfast the next day. But then again, he had to be hungry, and there weren't many other mealtime options in this neck of the woods.

She couldn't help noticing that he didn't look nearly as handsome as he had before. His hair was mussed as if he'd raked his hand through it a hundred times, and dark circles under his eyes suggested he hadn't slept a wink.

Was he worried about his sister? Had she gone into premature labor?

Lainie certainly hoped not. She didn't want Kara to lose her baby or to suffer any more than she already had.

Still, Drew looked worn. Tired. Uneasy.

She'd like to think his haggard appearance had to

do with guilt for being so mean to her last night, but his tight-lipped scowl told another story. Clearly, he hadn't softened toward her at all.

Only yesterday, he'd smiled as she bustled about, checking on the older men in the dining room, as well as the young hands who ate in the kitchen. He'd seemed to take pleasure in her movements. But today, as she served the men, replenishing their cups with fresh coffee and putting warm biscuits, butter and honey on the table, he didn't seem to notice her at all.

No, things had clearly changed between them—and permanently, it seemed. His frosty silence was pretty convincing.

As she continued to work, she did her best to ignore both him and his grumpy expression. But it wasn't easy.

She'd considered looking for a replacement to cover for her until Joy returned from her honeymoon and took over the kitchen duties. But Lainie couldn't leave before the party. The invitation had already gone out to Kidville, and there was no way she'd do anything to disappoint Andre or the other children. So she was determined to soldier on and see it through, at least until Christmas.

Besides, pouring herself into the party plans, baking cookies and creating inexpensive, homemade decorations would keep her busy and, hopefully, ease her heartache.

"These buttermilk biscuits sure are good, ma'am," Brad said.

Lainie thanked him. "Would you like another? I have more warming in the oven."

"No, ma'am. I've already had three and filled my belly to the brim. If I don't quit now, I won't be able to move, let alone work."

As the men began to push away from the table, she placed her hand on Drew's shoulder to stop him. "Can we talk a minute?"

His corded muscle tensed, and his eyes narrowed, creasing his brow. In some ways, his suspicion and distrust hurt her more than if he'd said, "There's nothing to talk about," and stomped off with the others.

"It won't take but a minute," she said.

He neither agreed nor objected, but he remained in his seat while the ranch hands filed out of the kitchen, into the mudroom and then out the door.

Once they were alone, she pulled out the chair next to him and asked, "How's your sister?"

Apparently he hadn't seen that question coming because the furrow in his brow deepened. "She's all right, I guess. It didn't help her to flip out after seeing you with me in the cabin."

Ouch. Yet in spite of the painful barb, she wasn't going to cower or apologize for something that had been all Craig's fault and none of her own doing.

"I'm glad to hear she's okay," she said.

His only response was a slight nod.

"I meant what I told you last night. I had no idea Craig was married. If I had, I would've run for the hills. Granted, I should have done a background check of some kind, an internet search of his name, but I didn't.

It won't happen again, though. I'll be more careful and skeptical from now on. And just for the record, I regret not checking up on you, too. I really should have, but I guess there's no need to anymore."

His eye twitched, but he didn't comment. If she were one to resort to violence, she might have shaken him until his teeth rattled. Instead, she pushed away from the table, standing tall, head high, her tears in check. "Someday, you're going to want someone's understanding and forgiveness, and I hope you get it."

"Maybe I won't deserve it."

She took a deep breath, wondering why she was wasting her time on him. Misplaced hope and a romantic delusion, she supposed, but her feelings and disappointment weren't the only things to consider. She had the Hoffmans and the children to think about.

"Do you still plan to support Kidville?" she asked.

"I told you I would."

"Yes, but I thought you might have changed your mind during the night. Of course, it's clear you haven't changed your opinion about me."

When he didn't respond, not even with a telltale blink of the eye, she bit down on her bottom lip, struggling with what to say next. They obviously didn't have a romantic future together, but they still had to cross paths.

"I realize there isn't a snow cone's chance in hell of us becoming friends," she said, opting not to use the word *couple*.

"And just so you know, I didn't ask you to stick around after breakfast so I could convince you otherwise. But we have a party to get through. Can we strike some kind of a cordial truce until I leave the ranch?"

"Sure, we can do that."

She let out the breath she'd been holding, relieved that they might be able to put things behind them. Yet, for some reason, it was important for him to know that she had a loving heart and good intentions.

"I'm going to adopt Andre and his brothers," she said. "Or if that doesn't come together for some reason, I'm going to take them in as foster children."

His response was sharp and immediate. "Are you kidding? How are you going to do that? You can barely support yourself and don't have a home. Why would you subject kids to an uncertain life?"

Lainie wasn't sure what hurt worse—his sharp tone or his lack of compassion. She never should have shared her innermost hope with a man who clearly didn't trust her or care about her feelings.

Sure, Drew had a point. She couldn't very well bring three young children into her life until she found a full-time job and a bigger place to live than a studio apartment. But she wasn't going to be bullied, hurt or taken advantage of any longer, especially by the likes of Craig or Drew.

Instead of fingering her scar and retreating, as she'd been prone to do in the past, she rose up to him and lifted her finger, jabbing his chest. "You're a self-centered jerk. You might not think so, but you're not any better than Craig Baxter. First you hurt my feelings, then you insult me."

As Drew gaped at her, his surly expression morphed into one of surprise.

"Cat got your tongue?" she asked, her own ire rising at a deafening speed.

"There's really not much to say."

"You're right."

She'd never wanted to clobber anyone so badly in her life, other than her drunken father. But he'd died in a barroom brawl when she and Rickie were seven, so she hadn't had to rise to the occasion. Besides, she'd never resort to violence, even if Drew made it oh so tempting.

"To make it easier for both of us," she said, "I'm going to try and find a temporary cook to cover for me until Joy returns. Either way, I'll stay out of your way until after the party. Then, by hook or crook, I'm going to create a home for Andre and his brothers. And you mark my words, I'll pull that off, or I'll die trying."

Then she turned on her heel and marched off, her head held high, but her heart and soul aching.

Drew stood alone in the kitchen, stunned by Lainie's anger and spunk.

Okay, so maybe he'd been an ass and deserved a good tongue-lashing after his gut reaction to her announcement that she intended to adopt not one, but three kids.

Her family plan was probably heartfelt, but so was Drew's response. He hadn't meant to come across so harsh, but she wasn't the only one thinking about the kids.

To this day he remembered going to bed hungry

as an adolescent, his belly empty and growling. After his mom got sick and could no longer work, money was tight and food was scarce, especially at the end of the month when her disability check ran out. So Drew often took less than his share at mealtimes to make sure his mother was able to keep up her strength and his sister had enough to eat.

Andre and his siblings might be separated, but at least they had warm beds and full stomachs at night.

Lainie couldn't blame him for connecting the dots to her living situation. She'd made it clear that she needed to find another job and another place to live. It didn't take a rocket scientist to realize she lacked the resources to provide for herself, let alone a family. What had she been thinking?

He supposed she'd been thinking with her heart. And that being the case, he had to admit that he and Kara might be wrong about her. Needless to say, he'd have to apologize to her, but he had some things to sort through before he chased after her.

The old-style ranch telephone, which hung on the kitchen wall, rang a couple of times. The nurses had their own phone back in the office, so it wasn't a call for them. Still, Drew doubted it was for him and waited for the answering machine to kick on.

When it did, a man's voice filled the room. "Lainie! It's Stan Carlton at *The Brighton Valley Gazette*. I've got good news, girl. I love that story proposal and want you to get started on it right away. And what's more, the Dear Debbie readership has grown impressively since you took it over. You're doing a great job. I can't wait to hear what the readers have to say when your next column comes out on Friday. Give me a call back at your convenience and we can talk about a raise in pay."

What the hell? Just about the time he thought he'd have to apologize for being a jerk, he hears this?

Lainie had lied to him. She'd told him that she hoped to land a job with *The Gazette*, but she already had one.

To top it off, she'd proposed an article, and it had been accepted. Did she have something underhanded in the works? Something that might exploit the old cowboys on the Rocking Chair Ranch or the children living at Kidville?

Dammit. Rather than offering up an apology, he was going to confront her with her lie.

Lainie tossed her freshly washed bedsheets into the dryer, albeit with a little more force than necessary. There was no point in taking out her anger, frustration and pain on the damp cotton percale, but it did help her work off some steam.

"There you are," Drew said from the doorway, his voice terse and not the least bit remorseful.

She glanced over her shoulder. "What do you want? Did you have more cruel barbs to sling at me, more false accusations to make?"

He leaned his shoulder against the doorjamb and crossed his arms. "Just one. You lied to me."

At that, she slammed the dryer door shut, turned to face him and slapped her hands on her hips. "How do you figure?"

"Stan Carlton from *The Gazette* called and left a message for you."

"What'd he say?"

"That your proposal was accepted, the Dear Debbie column is going great and that he's giving you a raise."

Finally. Some good news for a change. For a moment, she was so stunned—and pleased—that she forgot Drew had called her a liar. Well, more or less.

"You told me that you wanted to get a job at *The Gazette*," he said, "but apparently you already have one."

"Actually, it was a part-time position as the lovelorn columnist, and it didn't pay squat."

"You?" he said. "What do you know about love, let alone offering advice to people?"

"Not much, but thanks to Sully, I'm learning to problem solve."

Drew pushed away from the doorjamb and straightened. "What's that mean?"

"It's really none of your business. And you probably won't believe me anyway. But I needed to get my foot in the door at the paper, so I took the Dear Debbie position. Since I was at a loss on how to respond, I ran a few problems by Sully, who has more kindness, common sense and understanding of people in his little toe than you have in your big ol' cowboy body."

"You mean you don't have a bunch of troubled friends?" he asked.

She scrunched her face. "I have plenty of friends— smart ones. Nice ones from good families. But we all went different directions after college, and I'm new in Brighton Valley. I haven't made any local ones yet. Except for the men who live here."

"What about the article you proposed? What's that all about?"

What was this, the third degree? She wanted to tell him to take a very long walk off a short pier, one that stretched over shark-infested waters. But lashing out wasn't going to help much. She needed vindication.

"I proposed a big Sunday spread about the rodeo, the ranch and the children's home in hopes of gaining financial support."

His expression softened. Apparently, he'd begun to realize his assumptions and accusations might have been wrong. "I owe you an apology."

"Yes, you do. But right now, I'm not so sure I want to accept it." She turned around, set the dryer on high and pushed the start button.

When she turned around, he was still standing in the doorway, blocking her exit.

"Excuse me," she said. "I have work to do."

He stepped aside to let her out, and she marched off to find something to do. There was no point in arguing with a man who would never accept her for who she was.

Drew might not have faith in her, but she had faith in herself. Whether he believed it or not, she was going to help Andre reunite with his brothers. And somehow, in the process, she'd finally have a family of her own.

Chapter Twelve

Over the next couple days, Drew kept to himself, but by Friday, his niggle of guilt grew to a steady throb in the chest. He'd been wrong about Lainie, but he had no idea what to do about it.

He could tell her he was sorry, and she might accept his apology. But what about Kara? She wasn't apt to be as understanding or forgiving. And if not, that would really complicate his life.

Before breakfast, Drew climbed into his pickup and drove several miles down the road to the mom-and-pop market, where some of the locals hung out to while away the time and shoot the breeze. Once he'd parked in front, he entered the store.

A tall, wiry clerk sitting behind the register looked

up from the crossword puzzle he'd been working and smiled. "Howdy. Just let me know if I can help."

Drew sniffed the warm air. "Is your coffee fresh?"

"Sure is." The clerk got to his feet. "I just made a new pot. Can I get you a cup?"

"Yes, large. Black and to-go."

"You got it. Want a donut to go with that?"

Why not? He hadn't eaten breakfast. "Chocolate, if you have it."

As the clerk took a disposable, heat-resistant cup from the stack and filled it, Drew asked, "Do you carry *The Brighton Valley Gazette?*"

"You bet." The clerk pointed a long arm to the left of the register. "It's a dollar."

Drew retrieved the newspaper from the rack and returned to the register for his order. He paid with a twenty, pocketed his change and returned to his truck.

Instead of going back to the ranch, he settled in the cab, opened the small-town paper and searched for the Dear Debbie column.

There it was. Right next to the obituaries.

He took a sip of coffee, which hit the spot, then read the first of two letters. It was written by a woman who'd been taken in by a lying boyfriend. But it was Lainie's response that drew his interest.

I know exactly how you feel. It's painful to learn that a man you thought was Mr. Right lied to you—or even worse, that he doesn't trust you. And if that's the case, he's not the hero you thought he was.

Lainie must be referring to Craig's deceit, but Drew had hurt her, too. He was the one who hadn't believed her. So he wasn't feeling very heroic right now.

He continued to read the next letter. The writer was a woman who'd gotten angry with her family and, on principle alone, refused several of her sister's attempts to make amends. Just as he'd done moments before, Drew focused on Lainie's response, which was especially personal—and telling.

> *My own family was far from perfect. After my mom died, my sister and I were raised by an alcoholic father who couldn't keep a job. Needless to say, life was far from easy.*
>
> *Not long after my seventh birthday, my dad died in a bar fight, and my sister and I were placed in foster care. I'd been suffering from several medical problems that had never been addressed, one of which was life-threatening and required surgery, so the state stepped in and split us up. We ended up in different homes, and she was adopted. I haven't seen her since.*
>
> *Forgive me for not feeling very sympathetic to your anger or your plight. I lost the only family I had, and you're willing to throw away yours. Please reconsider. Love and forgiveness are powerful gifts. But even more so to the person who offers them freely.*

A pang of sympathy balled up in Drew's chest. He grieved for the child Lainie had been, yet he admired the woman she'd become. How could he have forgotten the kindness she showed the retired cowboys or the compassion she had for Andre and his brothers?

He didn't deserve a woman like her, but he wanted her in his life—if it wasn't too late. Yet he didn't move. He continued to sit in his pickup, staring at the newspaper in his hand without reading another word.

With each beat of his heart, he realized it wasn't just admiration he felt for Lainie. He loved her. Somehow, he had to make things right with her. And between her and Kara, too.

So he started the engine and headed back to the ranch. When he arrived, he spotted an unfamiliar car parked in the yard and Lainie walking out onto the front porch, her curls softly tumbling along her shoulders. She wore a somber expression and carried both a suitcase and a purse.

Panic rose up from his gut, and he crossed the yard to meet her. "Where are you going?"

"Back to town."

"What about the Rocking Chair Ranch? The men need you." Drew needed her. "What about your job?"

She didn't even blink. "I found a woman to cover for me until Joy gets home. I'll be back for the party."

Drew had no idea how to bridge the rift he'd created between them, but he had to give it his best shot. "Before you go, I want to apologize."

She studied him for a moment, then gave a slight shrug. "Okay. You're forgiven."

So she said. But Drew couldn't read an ounce of

sincerity in her expression or in her tone. And he really didn't blame her.

"Can we talk privately?" he asked. "It's important."

She continued to stand there, gripping the handle of her bag and clutching her purse. For a moment, he thought she was going to refuse. Not that he wouldn't deserve it if she did.

He reached for her suitcase without actually taking it from her. "Please?"

She sucked in a deep breath, then slowly blew it out and handed him her bag. "All right. But just for a minute."

He scanned the yard, spotting several ranch hands coming out of the barn and a couple of the old cowboys rocking on the porch. "Let's go to my cabin. I'd rather not have an audience."

She fell into step beside him as they crossed the yard to the cabin. Minutes later, he opened the front door ahead of her and waited for her to enter. Then he joined her in the small living area and set down her bag near the sofa.

"I've been a jerk. I assumed the worst about you, and in that sense, I didn't treat you any better than Craig did." When she didn't object, he continued. "I've seen you with the elderly men, watched as you served them meals and laughed at their jokes. And I've seen you with Andre. You've got a good heart, and only a blind fool would've missed that."

Her expression softened a tad, and she ran her hand through her glossy curls. "I told you that I forgave you."

"Yes, but you really didn't mean it then. Do you now?"

The corner of her lips quirked, revealing the hint of a smile. "Yes, I suppose I do. But it was more than just your distrust and lack of faith in me that hurt. You questioned my competency as a journalist, and…" She clamped her mouth shut as if having second thoughts about going into any more detail than that.

"Again," he said, "I'm sorry. There's so much about you that I admire. I'd really like to start over."

Her brows knit together. "In what way?"

"It would be great if we could roll back the time to when you offered me that sugar cookie. Or when the wagon's tailgate broke."

She didn't seem to see any humor in that suggestion.

"Let's just start at an hour before that call with my sister the other night."

"When we were in the kitchen?" she asked.

"Yes. If we were to start again there, I'd take you outside on the porch with me. Then I'd ask about your early years. And I would've really listened. I would have admitted that it broke my heart to think of you losing touch with your twin."

A tear spilled down Lainie's cheek, and she swiped it away with the back of her hand and sniffled. "Rickie was my only sister, my only family."

The reason he'd wanted to backpedal was to introduce her to Kara in another way, a better one.

"I have a sister, too," he said, "and she's my only family. She's pregnant and going through a divorce."

Lainie blinked back her tears. "I didn't realize Craig was…"

Drew placed his index finger on her lips to halt her explanation. "I believe you, Lainie. And I should have from day one."

"It's weird," she said, her voice as soft as a whisper. "People think I went after him, but it's the other way around. I'd been reluctant to date him at all. Looking back on it now, I realize that I'd always craved having someone to love, and he picked up on that need and used it to his advantage."

"Craig's a womanizer," Drew said. "And apparently, he's pretty damn good at it."

Lainie shrugged. "I'd only met him two weeks before—at a coffee shop next to the office where I'd worked at a temp job after graduation. He picked up the tab, and we chatted awhile. I don't normally talk to strangers, but when he told me he was nursing a broken heart and grieving a failed marriage, I felt sorry for him.

"When he asked me out the next day, I agreed to meet him for lunch at a nearby deli. He asked about my sun sign, which should have been my first clue that he was a player. But I went along with it and mentioned that my birthday was coming up. He surprised me by having a gift delivered to the office—a red dress and an invitation to meet him at Sterling Towers for a birthday dinner. I'm sure you know the rest."

"Pretty much."

"It rankles me now, but I went. But I wouldn't have if I'd known what was going to unfold."

"Kara found you together," Drew supplied.

Lainie nodded. "She'd been crying, and she stormed to our booth and asked Craig what in the hell was going on. He told her, 'Nothing,' and called her 'sweetie' and insisted I was 'nobody.'"

"I'd like to punch his lights out," Drew said.

Lainie smiled. "For a moment, I thought your sister was going to do just that. Instead, she snatched the margarita I'd been drinking and splashed the rest of it in my face. I don't know what stung worse, the icy cold on my skin, the humiliation or hearing Craig call me a 'nobody.'"

Drew's heart ached for Lainie. And for a lot of reasons—Craig's deceit, Kara's blame, the rumors that claimed Lainie was a villainess.

"Several diners held up their cell phones," Lainie said, "recording the ugly scene. And before I knew it, I became the night's social media entertainment."

"I'll explain all of this to my sister," Drew said. "She'll get over it. Eventually."

"That's okay," Lainie said. "I doubt that she and I will ever see each other again."

As a tear spilled over and trailed down her cheek, Drew brushed his thumb under her eye, wiping it away. Then he cupped her face with both hands and gazed at her. "Sure, you'll see her. That is, if you'll give me a chance to prove myself and go out with me."

Drew was asking her out on a date?

Lainie hadn't seen that coming. "Seriously?"

"You bet I am. My sister will get over blaming you, especially if I vouch for you."

This conversation wasn't at all what she'd expected. As she pondered his words and let them settle over her, she kept quiet.

Drew's thumb made a slow circle on her cheek, singeing her skin. "I've never met anyone like you, Lainie. I never expected to. And now that I have, I've rethought the future I'd laid out for myself."

To include her? She wasn't about to make a leap like that. "I don't know what to say."

"Tell me you'll let me show you that I'm a much better man than Craig."

"You've already proven that a hundred times over."

Drew brushed his lips against hers in a whisper-soft kiss that stole her breath away.

She was tempted to lean into him, to wrap her arms around him and let him take the lead, but she rallied. "First, before you say anything else, there's something I need to tell you."

His hands slipped from her jaw to her shoulders, but he didn't remove his touch, didn't remove his heated gaze. He didn't even blink. "Fire away."

He trusted her to lay everything on the line?

She sucked in a fortifying breath, then slowly let it out. "When I was a kid, I used to get tired doing the simplest things. But no one ever cared enough to worry about me or take me to the doctor. If they had, my congenital heart defect would have been diagnosed and corrected sooner. As it was, I didn't have surgery until I was eight."

"And that's when you lost touch with your sister."

She nodded. "It was a lonely, scary time. But don't get me wrong. I'm thankful that the state stepped in because then a skilled pediatric surgeon made me healthy. Things were better after that, but I was still very much alone and would have given anything for someone to love. At least, someone special."

"Has there ever been anyone special?"

"My college roommates, but we all went our separate ways. And there was one guy—for a little while. But he wasn't the man I thought he was."

"You mean Craig?"

"No, Craig was my second mistake. Right after I started college, I met a guy named Ryan and thought he might be 'the one,' but he wasn't. I can see that now. He kept pressuring me to have sex, but I wasn't ready. Then one night, I decided to give in, just to please him. But things never even got that far. It turned out badly, and we broke up."

"You don't have to talk about it—if you don't want to."

"I need to." It was the lead-in to what she had to tell him. "After I removed my blouse, Ryan froze up. You see, I have a long, ugly scar that runs along my sternum from my open heart surgery, and he was turned off by it."

"Oh, Lainie." Drew pulled her into his arms, holding her in a way she'd never been held.

She leaned into him, savoring his clean, woodland scent, his warm, comforting arms. "You're an amazing woman—beautiful, sweet, warmhearted. I don't want *you* to freeze up on me, but I'm falling in love with you. And there's nothing more I'd like than to take you to bed and show you just how much. But I'm a patient man. I'm willing to wait until you're ready."

Drew loved her? Could that be true?

She gently pushed against his chest, freeing herself from his embrace. "You haven't seen that scar yet."

"I don't need to." He pulled her back into his arms and kissed her long and deep. His tongue swept through her mouth, seeking and mating with hers until her knees nearly gave out.

She wanted to cling to him for the rest of her life, but she stopped the kiss before it was too late and took a step back. For once, she needed to let her head rule over her heart.

"Just so there aren't any surprises…" She unbuttoned her blouse, slipped it off her shoulders and dropped it onto the sofa. Then she unhooked her yellow satin bra and pushed the straps off her shoulders.

As she tossed it aside and stood before him, baring her flaw, his breath hitched. But not in revulsion. His expression was heated, fully aroused with desire.

"Aw, Lainie. You're beautiful."

Her hand lifted to her collarbone, a habit she couldn't seem to break, but he stopped her.

"Don't." He gently fingered the faded ridge, then bent his head and kissed the length of it. The warmth of his breath soothed her like a balm, healing the very heart of her.

He caressed the curve of her waist and along the slope of her hips, cherishing her with his touch, telling her without words that she mattered to him. Yet he was providing her with more than comfort, he was stirring her hormones and arousing her senses.

Her nipples hardened, and an ache settled deep in her core. When she thought she might die from pure sexual need, he pulled his lips from hers and rested his head against hers.

"I want to make love with you," he said. "But I won't press you until you're sure about me. About us."

She could hardly believe this was happening. "I'd like that, too. And to be honest, I'm ready now."

"You have no idea how glad I am to hear that. But are you sure?"

"It scares me to say this, but I love you, Drew. More than I ever dreamed possible."

He took her hand and led her across the small living area to the bedroom. "Is this your first time?"

She nodded. "I'm sure you're probably used to women with more experience—"

He squeezed her hand. "That's nothing to be sorry for. You're giving me a gift. And it's the best one I've ever had."

He removed his shirt and pants, while she kicked off her shoes and peeled off her slacks. Then he drew her into his arms again and kissed her, caressing her and taunting her with his skilled touch.

Lainie took the time to explore his body, too. Her fingers skimmed his muscular chest, the broad width of his back.

Drew trailed kisses along her throat and down to her chest. Then he took a nipple in his mouth, suckling it, lavishing one breast then the other. She moaned, unable to stand much more of the amazing foreplay.

Before she melted to a puddle on the floor, Drew lifted her in his arms and placed her on top of the bed. He joined her, and they continued to kiss, to taste and stroke each other until Drew pulled back and braced himself up on his elbow. "This might hurt the first time."

"I know. And it's all right." She'd been waiting for Drew—and for this—all of her life.

He entered her slowly at first, letting her get used to the feel of him, the feel of them, until he broke through. It stung, and her breath caught as she gave up her virginity, but her body soon responded to his, taking and giving. Loving and being loved.

As they reached a peak, she cried out, arched her back and let go. An amazing, earth-shattering climax set off an overwhelming burst of love and a sense of absolute completion.

When it was over, they lay still, basking in a sweet afterglow.

Moments later, Drew rolled to the side without letting her go. "It'll be better next time."

"I thought it was pretty amazing now."

He brushed a loose strand of hair from her brow, then traced her scar with his finger, gently and almost reverently. "Don't ever hide this again. Not from me or from anyone. It's a part of the miracle of *you*. Without that surgery, you might not have been here to meet me, to love me."

"You're right. I'm still trying to wrap my mind around it."

"Me, too," he said. "I never expected this to happen, but I can't imagine my life without you in it. I want to marry you—but only when you're ready."

Her heart soared. Christmas had come early this year. For the first time ever, Lainie had a real future stretched out before her and the promise of the family she'd never thought she'd have.

Only it wasn't that simple.

"I might have a deal breaker," she said.

"What's that?"

"I want to apply to be a foster parent so I can take Andre and his brothers. I don't like the idea of them being separated. I realize the state might find me lacking. But I'm determined to do whatever it takes to get those kids into the same home—either mine or in another where someone will love and care for them."

Drew slowly shook his head. She waited for his objection, but instead, one side of his mouth quirked in a crooked grin. "I have to admit that getting a wife and family in one fell swoop was never on my radar, but a lot's changed since I met you."

"You mean you're up to being a foster dad?"

"I am if we're in this thing together. Hell, maybe we can help find more foster families or adoptive parents in the area."

Her breath caught and excitement built as the wheels began to churn in her mind. "We can create a blog, highlighting kids who need forever homes."

Drew laughed. "Maybe we've found a higher calling than rodeos and advice columns."

"That's true. But my biggest and highest calling is you. I love you, Drew." Then she kissed him, sealing those words the only way she knew how.

The Christmas party had been a huge success, and everyone seemed to have had a great time.

Joe and Chloe Martinez, the ranch owners, arrived earlier that morning and had been pleased at how Lainie had pulled things together in such a short period of time.

"I had a lot of help," she'd told them.

Drew had purchased the tree, as well as the ornaments. And the retired cowboys had all pitched in to help him with the decorating.

Molly, Brad's mother, had slipped away from Kidville several different evenings to help Lainie with the baking. They'd also wrapped all the presents and placed them under the tree.

Sully had returned a few days ago with his brother Homer, a happy-go-lucky fellow who seemed to fit right in with the other retired cowboys. As soon as Homer unpacked his things, he'd jumped right in to party mode, offering his help whenever needed. So Lainie had gladly put him to work.

While Homer made himself useful by decorating the tree, wrapping gifts and frosting sugar cookies, Sully practiced his ho-ho-ho to perfection. The wise old man was a natural Santa as he chatted with the children and passed out candy canes.

Lainie couldn't believe how well the party turned out. Or how many great photo ops she'd had that day.

There'd been a few disappointments, though. Andre's brothers had yet to arrive. And Kara, who'd been invited, hadn't been able to come because she was still taking it easy. But she'd invited Drew and Lainie to her house to spend Christmas Day. Somehow, Drew had convinced Kara to give Lainie a chance. Lainie hoped they'd be able to get past the whole Craig fiasco, and Drew insisted they would.

Dark clouds had gathered all morning, and the rain began just before noon, so they'd canceled the hayride and rescheduled it for a warmer, drier day.

Now, as the party was coming to an end, the children sat amidst torn wrapping paper and open boxes, admiring their gifts and munching on cookies. Lainie was glad she'd been able to offer them a few hours of fun.

"Congratulations," Drew said. "Things didn't go exactly as planned, but from the looks on those little faces, the party's been a huge success."

"Thanks, but I couldn't have done it without your help."

When he slipped his arms around her, she leaned into him and rested her head on his shoulder.

"I have a present for you," Drew said.

"You didn't have to do that." Just having him in her life, sharing his bed and loving him was gift enough for her.

"I've been working on it for a week, and…" He

glanced out the window and grinned. "Looks like it just arrived."

Lainie wasn't sure what he was talking about, but moments later a knock sounded at the door. Jim Hoffman, who'd been standing nearby, opened it for a petite woman and two small boys.

It had to be the social worker, along with Andre's brothers. But why would Drew say he'd been working on getting them here all week? She'd been the one to invite them. "Come on in," Jim said. "I'm glad you finally made it, Mrs. Tran." Then he called out, "Andre. Look who's here."

The boy, who'd been reading his new cowboy book, broke into a happy smile and shrieked, "Mario! Abel!" He scrambled to his feet and hurried to the door, his limp hardly noticeable.

The boys greeted each other with hugs and kisses.

"That's *my* present?" she asked Drew. "Looks like it's Andre's."

"It's the paperwork in Mrs. Tran's folder that's your gift," he said.

Bewildered, Lainie cocked her head and looked at the man she loved. "I don't understand."

"Congratulations, foster mommy. It's a boy. Actually, it's three of them."

Lainie's jaw dropped. "Are you kidding? They're going to let me take them? I… Well, my little studio apartment is going to be cramped, but I'll make it work. Somehow."

"No need." Drew reached into his back pocket and pulled out a folded sheet of paper. "I just signed a lease for a three-bedroom house in Wexler. It'll have to do for now."

"You did that for me?"

"I did it for *us*. Kids need a daddy, too. Don't you think?"

"Drew Madison, you're amazing. Have I told you lately that I love you to the moon and stars?"

"Just this morning, but I'd like to hear it again." He tossed her a dazzling smile.

"I plan to tell you every single morning and night for the rest of our lives."

"I have one last gift for you," Drew said.

"What more can you give me? My gosh, look at them. Their reunion is heartwarming. And so is their excitement." She pointed to the tree, where the three adorable brothers gazed up at the twinkling lights in wide-eyed wonder. "This has been the best Christmas ever."

"It's just the first of many—and it's not over yet." Drew reached into his shirt pocket, withdrew a business card and handed it to her.

DISCREET SERVICES
Damon Wolfe, Owner

She studied it carefully. "What's this?"

"The guy I hired to find Rickie."

"But it was a closed adoption."

"Damon is the best of the best. He told me to leave it to him. If Erica "Rickie" Montoya can be found, he'll find her."

She looked at him, her eyes glistening with tears. "I can't believe this. Drew, this is the very best gift anyone could ever give me."

He held her in his arms and kissed her again. "That's nothing compared to the gift you are to me. Come on, honey. Let's ask the Hoffmans to take a picture of us and the boys so we can have more than a memory of our first Christmas together."

"Good idea."

Lainie had always found the holidays to be depressing. But not any longer. She couldn't wait to create more of her very own family memories from this day forward.

And next Christmas couldn't come too soon.

* * * * *

Will Elena be reunited with her long-lost sister?
Find out in the next installment of
ROCKING CHAIR RODEO
The new miniseries by
USA TODAY *Bestselling Author Judy Duarte*
Coming in July 2018

And catch up with everyone on the
Rocking Chair Ranch:

ROPING IN THE COWGIRL
THE BRONC RIDER'S BABY

And if you loved this book
Look for NO ORDINARY FORTUNE
Judy Duarte's contribution to
THE FORTUNES OF TEXAS:
THE RULEBREAKERS
On sale February 2018
Wherever Harlequin books and ebooks are sold.

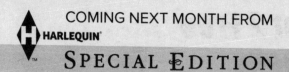

Get 2 Free Books,
Plus 2 Free Gifts—
just for trying the Reader Service!

"Why me—and why won't you take a hint that I'm just not interested?"

He stared into his single malt, neat, as if the answer to her question waited in the smoky amber depths. "I don't believe you're not interested. You just don't trust me."

"Duh." She poured on the sarcasm and made a big show of tapping a finger against her chin. "Let me think. I wonder why?"

"How many times do I need to say that I messed up? I messed up twice. I'm so damn sorry and I need you to forgive me. You're the best thing that ever happened to me. And…" He shook his head. "Fine. I get it. I smashed your heart to tiny, bloody bits. How many ways can I say I was wrong?"

Okay. He was kind of getting to her. For a second there, she'd almost reached across the table and touched his clenched fist. She so had to watch herself. Gently she suggested, "How about this? I accept your apology. It was years ago and we need to move on."

He slanted her a sideways look, dark brows showing

glints of auburn in the light from above. "Yeah?"

"Yeah."

"So then we can try again?"

Should she have known that would be his next question? Yeah, probably. "I didn't say that."

"I want another chance."

"Well, that's not happening."

"Yes, it is. And when it does, I'm not letting you go. This time it's going to be forever."

She almost grinned. Because that was another thing about Deck. Not only did he have big arms, broad shoulders and a giant brain.

He was cocky. Very, very cocky.

And she was enjoying herself far too much. It really was a whole lot of fun to argue with him. It always had been. And the most fun of all was finally being the one in the position of power.

Back when they'd been together, he was the poor kid and she was a Bravo—one of the Bastard Bravos, as everybody had called her mother's children behind their backs. But a Bravo, nonetheless. Nell always had the right clothes and a certain bold confidence that made her popular. She hadn't been happy at home by any stretch, but guys had wanted to go out with her and girls had kind of envied her.

And all she'd ever wanted was Deck. So, really, he'd had all the power then.

Now, for some reason she didn't really understand, he'd decided he just had to get another chance with her. Now she was the one saying no. Payback was a bitch, all right. Not to mention downright delicious.

THE WORLD IS BETTER WITH

Romance

Harlequin has everything from contemporary, passionate and heartwarming to suspenseful and inspirational stories.

Whatever your mood, we have a romance just for you!

Connect with us to find your next great read, special offers and more.

f /HarlequinBooks

@HarlequinBooks

www.HarlequinBlog.com

www.Harlequin.com/Newsletters

HARLEQUIN®

A *Romance* FOR EVERY MOOD™

www.Harlequin.com